A Harlequin Romance

OTHER

Harlequin Romances

by ELIZABETH ASHTON

1373—THE PIED TULIP
1421—PARISIAN ADVENTURE
1453—THE BENEVOLENT DESPOT
1534—COUSIN MARK
1636—FLUTTER OF WHITE WINGS
1659—A PARADE OF PEACOCKS
1713—ALPINE RHAPSODY
1741—MOORLAND MAGIC
1762—SIGH NO MORE
1788—ERRANT BRIDE
1810—THE ROCKS OF ARACHENZA
1835—DARK ANGEL
1853—THE ROAD TO THE BORDER
1869—THE HOUSE OF THE EAGLES
1891—SCORCHED WINGS

THE PLAYER KING

by

ELIZABETH ASHTON

HARLEQUIN BOOKS TORONTO WINNIPEG

Harlequin edition published October 1975

SBN 373-01918-1

Original hard cover edition published in 1975
by Mills & Boon Limited.

All the characters in this book have no existence outside the imagination of the Author, and have no relation whatsoever to anyone bearing the same name or names. They are not even distantly inspired by any individual known or unknown to the Author, and all the incidents are pure invention.

Printed in Canada

1918

CHAPTER ONE

DARK against the pageant of the sunset the coronet of crags on top of the mountain were a little sinister, they looked to Jocelyn Seymour like gigantic claws.

Accompanied by her father and brother, she had come from Edinburgh, which they had left that morning after arriving by motorail, and had spent an exhausting day visiting en route Stirling Castle, Loch Katrine and the Queen Elizabeth Forest, so she was feeling a little tired. After driving up the beautiful lakeside road along Loch Lomond, she was eagerly anticipating a wash and change before dinner at the hotel in Arrochar where they were spending a couple of nights. Crossing the neck of land at Tarbet which divides Loch Lomond from Loch Long, she had caught sight of what seemed to her to be a most unusual mountain.

'Ron, do you see that?' she cried. 'It's quite fantastic. What's it called?'

'Oh, that's Ben Arthur, commonly called the Cobbler,' her brother informed her, 'and those are the rocks Dad and I have come to climb. Looks as though they might be fun.'

Ronald Seymour was no stranger to Scotland where he had spent previous holidays, but it was his sister's first visit. She had not slept much during her night in the train, but excitement had buoyed her up until the long run beside Loch Lomond when, saturated with the sight of mountains, lochs and sky, she had been half asleep until the glimpse of the Cobbler had startled her to a new awareness of her surroundings.

'It seems sacrilege to call such an adventure merely fun,' she commented, 'and audacious to invade the privacy of the mountain tops.'

Her father, George Seymour, who was driving, laughed. 'You don't suppose they mind?' he asked. 'They're inanimate objects, my dear, and you're being fanciful. I expect you need your dinner.'

'Comes of being an actress,' Ron observed. 'You live in a makebelieve world, Jo. Thank goodness I've never been bitten by the acting bug. I've always been a down-to-earth sort of chap.'

He was referring to the fact that the Seymours were a theatrical family, being descended from an actor–manager who had run his own company. Vanessa Seymour had played small parts on stage and in television until she married her George when she retired. He was a stage electrician. Jocelyn had more talent than her mother had ever possessed and Vanessa had hoped to see her ambitions fulfilled in her daughter, but so far the girl had not progressed very far in her overcrowded profession. Ron had chosen more stable work—he was a car salesman.

Jocelyn had just completed a gruelling season in repertory, and had come home so exhausted, her father had insisted she must have a holiday before looking for another job, and had suggested she should accompany him on this Scottish trip. Though she did not climb, she could loll about at the hotels where they were to stay, and it would do her more good to get some bracing mountain air than to go with her mother to Bournemouth, where Vanessa was visiting relatives, which she found more congenial than Scotland. Jocelyn hated seaside resorts and being more in sympathy with her father than her mother had accepted with alacrity. Ronald, with brotherly candour, had stated he had no objection to her inclusion provided she did not grumble when they left her to go rock climbing.

'Oh, I won't mind,' she promised. 'There's certain to be some friendly people at the hotels, and I'll be perfectly happy doing nothing.'

So here they were arriving at Arrochar with the men's first objective in view. Later they proposed to go on to Fort William and tackle Ben Nevis.

George turned the car into the narrow road that ran along the side of the loch and slowed to a crawl as they looked at the grey stone buildings that fringed it.

'Here we are,' Ronald announced. 'That's it—the Highlander. Looks quite a superior sort of place. Been a bit reckless, haven't you, Dad?'

'I like good food,' his father returned comfortably, 'and I don't intend to stint on this holiday. It was recommended in the Guide. Plenty of porridge may put a bit of flesh on Jo's bones.' He glanced back affectionately at his daughter. 'She looks as though a strong wind would blow her away.'

'Ugh!' Jocelyn did not like porridge.

'Then plenty of bacon and eggs, none of your dried toast nonsense. I want to see you look blooming again.'

The long winter season of arduous duties as A.S.M. and a succession of small parts had taken the colour from Jocelyn's cheeks and reduced her natural slimness almost to emaciation. Her smoky blue eyes in their dark surround of lashes looked too big for her thin face, and the weight of her heavy hair, which she wore in a knot in the nape of her neck, seemed too great for its slenderness. It was rich auburn hair that looked black in shadow but in sunlight blazed with a dark fire. With her straight nose and full mouth she did not look modern but more like a Burne-Jones or Rossetti painting, but as her preference was for period plays, her appearance was an asset.

George brought the car to a halt on the tarmac parking space at the side of the hotel. A steep wooded bank rose up behind it, while it faced across the road to the loch and the gaunt mountains on its opposite shore.

Jocelyn climbed out of the rear seat feeling a little stiff, while her father went to get their cases out of the boot. The Cobbler's crest was just visible over the shoulder of a nearer mountain, and she wondered how it had got its name.

Jocelyn's room was on the top floor of the hotel, the others having a double room on the floor below. Adjacent to her room was the hotel's special feature, a sun lounge overlooking the loch. There before a huge window one could sit in an easy chair and absorb the beauty of mountain and loch without any effort or being teased by the wind. Jocelyn viewed it with delight. Here she could sit and lounge while Ron and George climbed their rocks, though they would be too far distant for her to be able to watch their progress.

She had arranged to meet George and Ron in the bar for an aperitif before dinner and she hastened to change from slacks and tank top into a dress after a welcome shower. She selected a dark blue dress with short sleeves and a square neck. It showed up the whiteness of her skin, which she viewed with some disfavour. Everyone else she had glimpsed that day seemed to have managed to acquire a tan.

'I certainly do look pale, and I hope interesting,' she said to herself, 'but it's not exactly becoming.' Defiantly she rubbed some colour into her wan cheeks and made up her mouth. She was pleased to see the false complexion had brightened her eyes.

Hers was the end room in the corridor that passed behind the sun lounge. There were several others and they all looked out on to the wooded bank behind the hotel. Rowan, beech and birch rose up to the skyline so that she was looking into a green bower, which was refreshing after the grimy street where her theatrical lodging had been situated. Not that she had taken much notice of her surroundings. Repertory entailed rehearsals of the next play while the current one was being played and all her days and nights had been spent in the artificial atmosphere of the theatre. It had absorbed her, but it had taken its toll of her energies and she felt a rush of gratitude towards her father for providing this peaceful and invigorating holiday which she needed.

She went down in the lift and made her way to the bar. George was wearing a jacket over his pullover, but Ronald had changed into a smart suit with a collar and tie. In appearance he was very like her, having the same colouring and small bones, and he could look very elegant. He was flirting negligently with the barmaid and Jocelyn smiled. Ron liked girls, but refused to be serious about any particular one. She suspected he had dressed up to kill if he found one to please his fancy, but even if she did, she would come second to his mountaineering.

She went to join him, climbing up on to a stool at the counter, and George ordered a Martini for her. The other occupants of the bar were mainly middle-aged people in casual clothes whose holidays were not ruled by the school term. They eyed the newcomers furtively and with the coolness British people assume towards strangers.

'Dull-looking lot,' Ronald said without bothering to lower his voice. 'I'm afraid you'll be a bit bored while we're out.'

'I couldn't be in such a lovely place, and perhaps someone more interesting will turn up.'

'You've got a hope,' Ron jeered.

She smiled serenely. 'I'm not worried.'

They went in to dinner and glanced round at their very ordinary-looking companions. An elderly Scotswoman was seated at the next table; Jocelyn discovered later her name was McTavish. She gave the young Seymours a half-hearted smile. Jocelyn's returning smile was frank and friendly.

'Be careful,' her brother whispered, 'she's the sort that thrives upon gossip. I bet she's got a tongue like a wasp.'

'Don't be so uncharitable,' Jocelyn rebuked him. 'She can't help being old and faded and I'm sure she's perfectly harmless—besides, what could she say about me?'

How misplaced her confidence was she was to learn at a later date.

They had reached the entrée, roast duck and orange sauce, before Jocelyn noticed the couple seated in the window at a table for two. The man had his profile towards her, his companion, a small boy of about seven or eight, his back. She could only see his close-cropped black head above his chairback and the vulnerable-looking nape of his childish neck. The man's face was familiar. She knew that broad forehead above the deep eye sockets, the straight nose and well-shaped passionate mouth, the square chin and proud carriage. He seemed to be listening to the child's prattle with a faint boredom, though an indulgent smile touched his carven lips from time to time.

Jocelyn rubbed her eyes. She must be mistaken. He could not be patronising this out-of-the-way Scottish hotel, though she had heard him say he was fond of Scotland and liked to escape there when he could. She said to George:

'That man in the window, doesn't he remind you of someone?'

Her father turned his head in the direction that she had indicated and gave a low whistle.

'If I didn't know it was impossible I'd say it was the great Dorian Armitage himself, but he'd never come here. The Côte d'Azur is more in his line—and with a child!' He laughed. 'No, I don't see Dorian acting as a nursemaid to a little boy, but that fellow's extraordinarily like him.'

George had worked at several theatres where Dorian Armitage had been the leading man. He had a great respect for his talent, for Dorian had genius, but little for the man himself; there were too many stories about Dorian's amours. A goodhearted fellow in many ways, generous to a fault, and in spite of his success he never put on airs, but he was not to be trusted with women. George, as a respectable married man, looked askance at such goings on.

'Must be his double,' Jocelyn said lightly. 'They say we all have one somewhere.'

Surreptitiously she watched the pair by the window throughout the remainder of the meal. There appeared to be no woman with them and a certain similarity between the shape of the two dark heads suggested they were father and son. She had never heard that Dorian Armitage was married, much less had a family, which went to prove this could not be he. Jocelyn had worked with Dorian for a few glorious weeks during the previous summer before she joined the repertory company. Aubrey Oliphant's spectacular production of *A Midsummer Night's Dream* had been put on out of doors in the grounds of a ducal estate to raise money for a relief fund. No expense had been spared and many rich philanthropists had subscribed to it, the principals giving their services free. The company consisted of a galaxy of famous stars and under no other circumstances would the great Dorian Armitage have consented to play Oberon, the part being too insignificant for him, but Aubrey had persuaded him to do it. The famous director was reported to have said:

'Oberon should be beautiful and inhuman. No normal man would play such a grotesque trick upon his wife simply to gain possession of an adopted child. But

Oberon could not bear to be thwarted of his whim. Dorian has the quality I need to make the Fairy King convincing, an arrogant ruthlessness disguised by devastating charm.'

Jocelyn had been fortunate enough to obtain a small part in this much advertised production, that of the singing fairy, for she had voice enough to sing when required. She was only one of a horde of fairies and elves unnoticed by the principals, but she had been on stage with Dorian and he had made an indelible impression upon her. She had only to close her eyes to visualise him as he had appeared, bare brown limbs—he wore only a leopard's skin—slender but muscular, one smooth shoulder naked, the gleaming circlet upon his forehead above flowing gold-dusted hair, the haughty pride of his bearing, the scornful curl of nostril and lip as he addressed his rebellious queen, above all his eyes, curious cat's eyes, neither green nor gold but a mixture of both with pupils that expanded and contracted according to his mood. He was Pan, a faun, Oberon, king of a realm of fantasy, not quite human as Aubrey wanted him to be.

The Titania was Esme Carr, dainty in filmy draperies which showed every line of her perfect body, but her loveliness was marred by occasional petulance, nor did she quite manage to suggest an elfin being. But she was the moon to Dorian's sun and her name had been linked with his throughout the production, for it was whispered that their connection was not confined to the stage, and it was not only charitable motives that had reconciled him to playing a minor role.

The weather was perfect during the whole fortnight. The garden of the great estate possessed a natural stage surrounded by trees and bushes. There had been special coaches run to bring spectators from afar and the place had been filled to capacity every night.

To Jocelyn the two magic weeks had been an idyll

of pastoral delight. None of it had seemed quite real, from the mornings when she woke in her rustic lodging to the culmination of the evening show. Roses and lilies from the nearby flower garden exuded scent which wafted across their stage, which could by a stretch of imagination be that of the wild thyme oxlips and nodding violets mentioned in the play. The gossamer forms of fairies and elves flitting among the dark foliage of trees and bushes seemed in their right element, for she was living in a faerie world.

According to robust Elizabethan humour, the trick Oberon plays upon his wife would be considered a great joke and it is necessary to the plot, but it was no joke in Dorian's hands. He brought to his interpretation of his role a vindictiveness that was spine-chilling.

'That's Dorian all over,' Jocelyn overheard the girl who was playing Helena, whose overtures Dorian had snubbed, say, 'Thwart him and he turns into a devil. I pity the woman he marries!'

Bedazzled by the glamour of him as she was, the words held no significance for Jocelyn. He was only giving to the part the inhumanity that Aubrey had insisted upon. That it might be an expression of some latent vindictiveness in his nature would never occur to her, nor did she anticipate ever knowing him well enough to discover if it were true. Regarding 'Helena', she thought she would only be too glad to be that pitied woman if she got the chance, but Dorian devoted himself entirely to Esme.

From afar, Jocelyn wove her young romantic dreams about his golden figure. She was fascinated not only by his physical beauty but his enigmatical personality; he was fantastic, out of this world. Each night in the warm summer dusk when the dying light was augmented by cleverly directed floodlighting, she followed Titania in palpitating expectancy for the moment of confrontation.

'Ill met by moonlight, proud Titania.'

He barred their passage, his bronzed limbs silvered by a blue spotlight, arrogant head held high, his musical, vibrant voice thrilling her to her innermost core.

Once, when she encountered him waiting to make his entrance after she had sung her song, he had complimented her upon her charming voice, and that was her golden moment, for though Esme treated the small-part people like dirt beneath her feet, Dorian was always courteous, though she doubted he would remember her from one moment to the next.

It was only a passing infatuation, a youthful crush engendered by the sensuous atmosphere of those summer nights, but all through her months of hard labour at the repertory theatre she had been unable to exorcise his image, so that although despising herself for her foolishness she had held aloof from the casual intimacies indulged in by her colleagues. Frigid, iceberg, prude were the epithets flung at her by would-be amorous swains, but she was indifferent. Only one man had the power to rouse her, and he was unattainable.

He continued to obsess her and the chance likeness in an unknown man brought her memories thronging back, and set her heart beating with unreasoning anticipation, for of course the man with the child could not be Dorian Armitage, though he had the same teasing smile. When he stood up and when and if she heard him speak, the illusion would be dispelled, but it was disconcerting to realise how strongly Dorian still ruled her imagination.

In spite of her watchfulness, Jocelyn did not see the stranger leave his table. Ronald had drawn her attention to a passage in the guide book and while her head was bent, he slipped out unobtrusively. Lifting it, she saw his place was vacant and all she glimpsed of him was a lithe slim figure disappearing through the swing door of the dining room. The overhead light shone on his dark head, glossy as a rook's wing.

Dinner over, the two Seymour men announced that they were going for a stroll to view the object of their expedition on the morrow. Jocelyn declined their somewhat perfunctory invitation to accompany them, saying she was tired. She intended to go up to her room to fetch a paperback with which she had provided herself, and spend a quiet couple of hours in the sun lounge before going to bed.

Upon her arrival on the top floor she found the lounge deserted and paused for a moment to look at the view. The sun had sunk behind the hills though the sky was still luminous, and the Cobbler with adjacent hills were humped silhouettes against it. The waters of the loch reflecting the last of the light shone like pewter.

She became conscious of a thin, mewling sound, which she thought must be a cat or a puppy until she realised it was made by a child. She went through into the corridor behind the lounge and was able to locate it. It came from the last room in the corridor, the one furthest from her own and next to the swing door by which she was standing. The thin wail had been succeeded by muffled sobbing.

Impulsively she tapped upon the door, and receiving no response, pushed it ajar, for it was not locked. She found herself in a double room with a window looking out of the side of the hotel towards the head of the loch. In one of the twin beds she discerned a tousled black head and the huddled figure of a child, its face buried in the pillow. An anguished voice murmured: 'Nounou, oh, Nounou!'

Gently she asked:

'Do you want your mother, little one? Shall I fetch her?'

The bedclothes were flung back, and the child—she saw now it was a boy—sat up and stared at her with a woebegone expression.

'You can't, she's dead,' he told her bluntly. He had a faintly foreign intonation.

'Oh, my dear, I'm so sorry,' Jocelyn cried contritely. 'I'd no idea!'

She was almost certain he was the child she had seen in the dining room with the man who had intrigued her. If so he must be a widower and she felt a flicker of indignation. It was not very kind to leave the little boy alone at the top of a strange hotel while he amused himself, but perhaps he did not know the child was not asleep.

The black eyes in the small brown face were eyeing her suspiciously.

'*Alors*, who are you, *mademoiselle*?' he demanded.

'I'm staying here too,' Jocelyn explained. 'You seem unhappy, and I wondered if I could help.' The boy's lip quivered and she went on quickly. 'I saw you at dinner—was that your father with you?'

'Yes, that was *mon papa*,' the boy confirmed. French, Jocelyn wondered, or only partly so? 'Please do not tell him I was crying,' he went on anxiously. 'He wants me to be *un brave homme*, like he is. Papa has no fear.'

Reluctant tribute sounded in the childish voice; evidently he admired his father, who perhaps expected too much of him.

'So you will be one day,' Jocelyn said soothingly. 'But you've some way to go, haven't you? You're not a man yet.'

'When I am I hope I shall be like Papa.'

'No doubt you will be. Will you be all right now, if I leave you?'

The child looked fearfully around the shadowed room.

'*Mademoiselle*, can you stay a little while?'

Jocelyn sat down on his bed, the boy was obviously scared. Taking one of his small brown hands in hers, she asked:

'Has something frightened you?'

He nodded. 'It is the Cobbler,' he whispered. 'He is up there on that mountain top and *il est très effroyable.*'

'But there's nothing there, dear.'

Falteringly he told her what had been related to him, probably in answer to a query about the name. The mountain was so-called because some folk with vivid imaginations had declared the rocks on its summit were the shape of a cobbler bending over his lathe. The boy had seen it against the flaming sunset and found the supposed figure sinister. Overtired, and overstimulated, he had fancied the cobbler had descended from his pinnacle and was 'coming to get him.' Papa was several floors below, Maman was in heaven and Nounou was left behind in France, so there was no one to protect him.

Jocelyn thought that if this were the real reason for the naming of the hill it was an absurd flight of fancy, and she explained patiently that it was only an inanimate crown of rock which her father and brother were about to climb on the morrow. Aware that she was trespassing in a strange man's bedroom, she was anxious to escape before she was discovered.

'You're not alone up here,' she pointed out. 'My room's just along the passage, and there'll be people coming up to the lounge next door. I can't stay here any longer, so don't you think you could go to sleep now?'

But the child clung to her hand, the coaxing smile he gave her was oddly familiar.

'Please, *mademoiselle,* stay a little longer,' he pleaded. 'I don't like this so strange place, so different from my home in France. That was a smiling land, but this Scotland frowns.'

A fanciful child, Jocelyn thought, as she asked:

'So you lived in France?'

'Yes, *mademoiselle*, in a place where they grow vines. Maman was always going to Paris, but I had Nounou, she had always been with me since I was a baby. But when Maman died, *mon papa* came for me. He said I was too big to need a nurse and took me away. He lives in Londres, that I liked,' the black eyes sparkled, 'there is so much life, but he says he needs the holiday in the fresh air, and it will do me good also. *Mademoiselle*, I do not enjoy the fresh air and all these mountains, and I want Nounou.'

A fresh burst of tears followed this declaration, and impulsively Jocelyn gathered the thin little body into her arms, stroking the silky black head. From what he had said, she deduced that his father had not lived with his mother and was almost a stranger to him, a somewhat awesome figure whom he admired but did not find sympathetic. He could not realise that his son was lonely, deprived and frightened, or he would not have left him, but she had no right to interfere. However she could not leave the boy in this state, she could only hope his emotion would tire him out and he would soon fall asleep.

A sudden blaze of electric light dispelled the gathering dusk. Jocelyn had not heard anyone come in, but now she saw a man standing at the foot of the bed regarding her with mingled anger and astonishment.

'May I ask what you are doing in here young lady, and by what right you've taken it upon yourself to mollycoddle my son?'

At the sound of his voice, Jocelyn's heart began to hammer. She would know its cadences anywhere, nor was there any mistaking the eyes staring at her, cat's eyes, greenly-yellow, fringed with dark lashes. An ordinary lounge suit, immaculate shirt and tie replaced the leopard skin, but the conventional garb could not disguise the untamed essence of him, an affinity with the natural elements that had made him seem so at home in the 'wood near Athens.'

For months she had dreamed of him, had lived again those enchanted evenings in the dusk of the ducal garden. She had imagined ways of meeting him again in different places, but never had she anticipated an encounter in a hotel bedroom with his son's trembling body in her arms. But wonderment at this fulfilment of her wildest fantasies was swamped by the reality of the child's need.

'I heard this poor mite crying his heart out,' she told him, 'so I came in to see what was the matter.'

'Seven years old and snivelling,' Dorian Armitage said scornfully.

Jocelyn's temper rose in the boy's defence.

'That's no great age,' she exclaimed indignantly. 'He tells me he's lost his mother,' Dorian's lip curled contemptuously, 'and his nannie, and he's been frightened by some silly story. You leave him alone on the top floor in a strange place and wonder that he cries!'

The boy raised his head from Jocelyn's shoulder and said reproachfully: 'I asked you not to tell.'

'I can see without being told,' his father pointed out, eyeing his tear-stained face, but he spoke gently. 'Now we'll have to wash your face again, and that's something you don't like. But first we'll say goodbye to your ... er ... babysitter.' He looked at Jocelyn coldly: 'I really don't see what business it is of yours, Miss whoever-you-are.'

'A child crying is everybody's business,' Jocelyn returned. She laid the boy back on his pillow. 'You'll be all right now, little one, now Daddy's come.'

She stooped to kiss him, and rather to her dismay, he wound his arms about her neck, refusing to let her go. Dorian gave an exclamation of impatience.

'Precisely, now Daddy's come,' he mimicked her with an edge to his voice. 'My son's been spoilt by that woman who reared him, she babied him, and I wish him to learn to be independent—besides,' a wicked glint showed in his eyes, 'this does happen to be my bedroom.'

The hot colour sprang to Jocelyn's face at this reminder, and she disengaged herself from the clinging arms. Standing up, she murmured an apology, and saw he was amused by her embarrassment.

'I've been invaded by far more flimsy pretexts,' he told her ambiguously, his glance frankly mocking her. 'Say goodnight to your good Samaritan, Dorry, and tell her you're not going to be a baby any longer.'

'Oui, mon père. Remercie, mademoiselle.'

'Dorry, do please speak English. You can when you want to. You must remember you're a British boy and I'm your father.'

Unable to repress her curiosity any longer, Jocelyn blurted out:

'I didn't know you were married, Mr Armitage.'

'Few people did,' he returned, 'and certainly not the press. So you recognise me?'

'I'm one of your fans.'

'Indeed? I rather hoped to escape notice in this remote place,' he said ruefully. 'Please don't blazon my identity abroad.'

A shrill voice from the bed announced: *'Mon père* est Dorian Armitage, *mademoiselle,* and I'm Dorian too, though I'm called Dorry. Papa is a very great actor.'

There was pride in the childish tones; though he might be in awe of his father, or perhaps because of that, he appreciated his fame.

'I know he is,' Jocelyn assured him, smiling. 'Believe it or not, I appeared with him once.'

'You did?' Dorian's interest quickened. For the first time he really looked at her, noticing the rich coils of her hair, the wide spaced smoky blue eyes. 'So you're in the profession too? But I can't recall ... and surely I should do, for yours is a face not easily forgotten.'

She flushed with pleasure and then scolded herself for her naïveté. Dorian was adept at empty compliments.

'You wouldn't have noticed me. It was in the open-air production of *The Dream* last summer. I was one of Titania's train, though I was distinguished by singing a solo.'

'You spotted snakes, etc.? I remember you now, you looked enchanting.'

She did not believe him, he was far too glib, and she knew he had not recollected her name, if he had ever known it.

'I'm Jocelyn Seymour,' she told him, 'commonly referred to as Jo.'

'What desecration of a pretty name,' he objected. 'I prefer it in full. Jocelyn, it suits you.'

'Thank you,' she said demurely, while the sound of it on his lips gave her a thrill; he had such a beautiful voice and every syllable was perfectly pronounced, but his diction was one of his professional assets.

'That was a very exotic show,' he went on reminiscently, seeming to have forgotten that he had asked her to leave his room. Actually he was standing between her and the door, hands thrust into his trouser pockets, his eyes flickering over her as if he were assessing her every point. 'I consider I was miscast.'

'No, you weren't,' she assured him quickly. 'You gave a quite original interpretation of the part, and looked supremely regal.' She tried to reconcile her recollection of Oberon with this suave, sophisticated, dark-haired man.

'The part didn't have much to it.' He laughed. 'You and I have been wrangling over a child, though Dorry's not a changeling. It's the same situation as that in the play. Aren't you afraid I may make you become enamoured of an ass?'

'No need for that, I relinquish all claims to Dorry.' She laughed a little uncertainly. There was a cruel glint in his eyes, that made her feel uncomfortable, as if he would enjoy heaping humiliation upon her. 'Anyway, I wasn't Titania.'

'More's the pity, you'd have made a better fairy queen than that affected piece who played it.'

She opened her eyes wide in surprise. 'But I thought you admired her.'

He shrugged his shoulders. 'Insipid,' he declared.

Jocelyn wondered if their romance had gone awry, since he seemed to be out of love with his charmer. But stage affairs rarely did last long and unbeknown to the cast he had been married. That brought her thoughts back to the child, and turning towards the bed she saw the long black lashes had descended over his eyes and he had fallen asleep with the suddenness that overcomes small children.

'He's dropped off,' she whispered.

Dorian looked at his son, then glanced round the room where his masculine possessions, brocade robe, silk pyjamas, slippers and ivory-backed brushes were in evidence together with sundry small garments belonging to Dorry. His eyes came back to rest on the slender girl, while his mouth curved satirically. Scorning to whisper, he said pointedly:

'You know how to seize your opportunities.'

'What do you mean by that?' Jocelyn asked, her low voice vibrant with anger. Was he implying that she had used Dorry's distress as a means whereby she could ingratiate herself with his father?

He did not answer, but his eyes held hers in a long intent gaze. They shone yellow in the electric light with a peculiar lambency. A shiver ran down Jocelyn's spine, but she could not turn her head. He held her as a snake fascinates a bird. Then he moved away with a light laugh.

'Shall we seek more suitable quarters?' he suggested. 'I think your kindness to my son deserves some recompense. May I give you a drink?' He went to the door, holding it open for her to pass.

'Thank you,' she murmured almost inaudibly, as she went by him. In every nerve she was conscious of him, so much so that her usually ready tongue was dumb.

'We can phone for one to be sent up to us,' he told her, as he followed her into the sun lounge, 'then we shan't be far from Dorry if he wakes again.'

So he was not indifferent to his son's woes.

'That's a very good idea,' she agreed.

The place was nearly empty, as most of the visitors preferred the bar once the sun had gone and darkness obscured the views. Jocelyn sat down a little self-consciously in an armchair while Dorian gave his order over the service phone. She saw in a corner Mrs McTavish sitting with another elderly dame apparently in close converse, with coffee cups in front of them. Vaguely she wondered if they had seen her come out of Dorian's room through the glass of the connecting door to the passage, and smiled to herself. That would give them something to talk about if so inclined, but secure in the knowledge of her innocence, she was not in the least perturbed.

CHAPTER TWO

A WAITER appeared in the sun lounge, bringing their drinks on a tray. He switched on the rest of the lights, bathing the big room in brilliance, and drew the brocaded curtains over the large windows shutting out the night and the loch. Mrs McTavish and her friend went out with a murmured goodnight and inquisitive glances. Dorian and Jocelyn were alone.

She sipped the sherry he had ordered for her feeling that she was in the midst of another summer night's dream. She could not really be sitting with the object of her devotion in a remote Highland hotel whence chance or coincidence had brought him. Presently she would wake up and find it had been another fantasy.

To make conversation, for she was conscious of a slight constraint between them born of mutual shyness, she told him Dorry's story about the naming of the Cobbler and asked if there was any truth in it.

'Someone has been exercising a very fertile imagination,' he commented, 'unfortunately in Dorry's hearing. I suspect the name is merely a corruption of the Gaelic An Gobaileach, which means the twin peaks.'

'I wish I'd known that to tell Dorry,' she exclaimed. She was secretly grateful to the instigator of the legend which had resulted in this encounter.

'I will, in the morning.'

Ben Arthur disposed of, he fell silent, and Jocelyn sought for another topic since he did not seem inclined to be chatty. Tentatively she enquired if he were staying long at Loch Long.

'A week or so. Arrochar is a good centre,' he told her. 'It's about time I saw some more of Britain. The Mediterranean sun is more reliable than the Scottish weather, but I thought I'd give it a trial. Besides, I want Dorry to become more anglicised. He's been living with a French couple who owned a vineyard. His mother dumped him there.' He paused, and Jocelyn made no comment, though she was eager to know more. He glanced at her doubtfully, then as if unable to deny himself the pleasure of unburdening himself, said bluntly:

'I didn't live with my wife, not after the first year, we weren't compatible.'

'Thank you for telling me. No one in the profession has any idea that you've been married.'

He laughed ruefully. 'When the marriage took place I was quite obscure.' He took a gulp of the whisky he had ordered for himself. 'When I became a success I saw no point in advertising it, since we were separated. We married too young, Elise was only eighteen and I was twenty. We met when I was playing in Paris, a visit by an English company, and married in haste. The impetuosity of youth!' He laughed again. 'Of course, as happens in our profession there were long separations when I was on tour. Elise hated England, she resented her pregnancy. Finally when Dorry was two, she went back to France to live. I thought it best to leave the child with her, but I'd no idea she wouldn't keep him with her. Jeanne was engaged as a nursemaid, and when she married, Elise boarded the boy with her. When I asked for news of him, she always implied that she was living with him. When she died I had no alternative but to bring Dorry home. He wasn't getting a proper education, and the woman Jeanne was doing her best to turn him against me.'

'But it must have been a tremendous upheaval for the boy,' Jocelyn pointed out. 'And I gather you were almost unknown to him.'

'To my shame, I should have kept in closer touch, and I couldn't leave him with Jeanne. This trip was my grandmother's idea. "Go away and get to know each other," she said. You know my grandmother, of course—Eleanor Mainwaring?'

'Everyone knows Dame Eleanor,' Jocelyn told him. Dorian came of a famous stage family on his mother's side and his grandmother was a renowned veteran in the theatrical world. His parents had perished in a motor accident while on tour in America and Eleanor had brought him up.

'She should have come with us,' he went on. 'I'm afraid I'm not very good with small children. I don't seem to be making any headway with Dorry at all.'

Jocelyn thought he was not going the right way to win the confidence of a nervous child, but she could not tell him so. She did suggest that Dorry was a sensitive, highly strung boy and would need understanding.

'Which you don't think I'm capable of giving him?'

'I didn't say that, but you'll need to be patient.'

'Not one of my virtues.' Abruptly he changed the subject. 'How long are you staying here, Jocelyn?'

The informality of the use of her name pleased her. She explained that her plans were fluid. Ronald and her father had come up for some rock climbing. The Cobbler might amuse them for a day or two but they were going on to Ben Nevis.

'Bit dull for you,' he commented. 'Or do you climb?'

She shook her head. 'I'm resting in both senses. I had a hard season in rep after *The Dream*, so I'm not looking for a job at the moment. I shall just lounge about.' She looked at him hopefully. 'I was just thinking I might stay here instead of going on to Fort William with them, it's quieter and this seems to be a nice hotel.'

He gave her a sharp look, while his lips curled sardonically. She flushed under his keen scrutiny, wondering if she had been too obvious. She had fully intended to go on with Ron and George until she had met Dorry, and Dorry's father. It had occurred to her that she might be able to help him with the child, but he might misunderstand her motive.

'You'd be bored here all on your own,' he remarked.

'I'll be on my own wherever I am, since I don't intend to scale Ben Nevis.'

'No, you've hardly the physique for mountaineering,' he observed indifferently. He lit a cigarette and leaned back in his chair, watching the spirals of smoke ascend, apparently having lost interest in her. Jocelyn's gaze was drawn to his handsome profile, the straight nose with its haughtily curved nostrils, the firm cleft chin. Suddenly he turned his head and their eyes met; it was a long questing gaze, as if they would test each other's sincerity. He said quietly:

'Perhaps if you do decide to stay on here you would lend a hand with my small son?'

It was what she had been hoping he would say, but she had an impression that there was something behind the innocuous request. An inner voice warned her that she would be unwise to become involved with Dorian Armitage who was far too attractive for a girl's peace of mind.

But I needn't become involved with him, she thought. All he'll expect me to do is to take Dorry off his hands when he wants more sophisticated amusement. It's the child I'm thinking about.

To him she said: 'I'd be delighted, but aren't you trying to wean him from his dependence upon feminine influences?'

'Perhaps I've been too drastic and he needs them in moderation,' he admitted. 'I want him to become wholly British. He'll be going to school later on, so it's essential he should adjust to English ways. I'll be obliged if you'll discourage him from speaking French, of course, and squash these rather morbid fancies he gets, like the one about the Cobbler. French peasants are a mass of folklore and superstitions. I've been very lax, I should have checked up on the way he was being brought up.'

'Is the Highlands the right place for him?' Jocelyn asked. 'The Gaels are full of superstitions too, and some of them are fey.'

'You're unlikely to meet many of those. At this time of year Scotland is lousy with tourists of all nationalities,' Dorian said lazily. His eyes still lingered on Jocelyn's face and figure, and she felt a sudden qualm. His reputation with women was by no means lily-white, and he had soon found consolation for his absent wife. Uneasily she was aware of how susceptible she was to his sexual lure. She would have to be very careful not to make a fool of herself, for though ordinarily she could not compete with the lovely women who sought his favours, he might in this isolated region consider she presented a temporary diversion. His directions regarding Dorry had been as impersonal as instructions given to a governess, but there was a glitter in the strange eyes studying her that was not impersonal at all.

'I shall be very glad to help Dorry in any way I can,' she told him primly, turning away from that too intent regard.

Dorian contemplated her averted face for some moments with a little mocking smile twisting his beautiful mouth, as if he were well aware of her disquiet.

'You mustn't let him become an imposition,' he said at length.

'He could never be that.'

'Small children can be fairly exigent,' he warned her. 'And you're on holiday too. Perhaps I can make it worth your while.'

'I'm not asking for payment!' she exclaimed indignantly.

'A labour of love, eh?' He was definitely mocking her now. He added meaningly: 'Payment can be in many kinds.'

Careful now, instinct warned her. She said composedly: 'If I can comfort Dorry for all he's lost that will be ample recompense.'

'You're easily satisfied, and I'm sorry you seem to think I've deprived my son,' he told her a little stiffly.

'I didn't mean that ... only ...' she floundered, 'he has lost his mother.'

'He's not grieving for her, my dear, and no more am I,' he proclaimed lightly. 'So you won't need to present yourself in a maternal capacity, it might lead to ... er ... misunderstandings.'

She clenched her hands. Was he hinting that she might aspire to take Elise's place?

'Such an idea was far from my thoughts.'

Dorian laughed with wholehearted enjoyment. 'I'm ungrateful to tease you,' he exclaimed. 'I don't really suspect you of any ulterior motive. You're just a goodhearted, goodnatured girl, who wants to befriend an orphan and a widower.'

'You can't need anyone to befriend *you,*' she stated frostily, nettled by his contemptuous tone which belied his words.

'But you are befriending me if you look after Dorry. I confess I'm finding fatherhood much less straightforward than I expected.'

Disarmed, she said gently: 'With his mixed parentage Dorry is possibly more complicated than a normal boy would be.'

The greeny-yellow eyes sparkled mischievously. 'Indeed?' he murmured, then added insinuatingly, 'Perhaps you'd understand him better if you made a study of his father.'

'That won't be necessary,' she said hurriedly, 'and I thought it was you who wanted to understand *him.*' She rose to her feet. 'It's time I went to look for *my* father, he'll be wondering where I've got to.'

She moved towards the door and Dorian sprang after her.

'You're not going to back out?' he asked anxiously. 'I really do need your help with Dorry.'

'I . . . I don't know. I'll think about it,' she said as she went towards the lift.

He caught her by her shoulders, and turned her to face him.

'Please, Jocelyn,' he murmured, exerting all his charm of face and voice. 'After all, it was in your mind before I mentioned it, wasn't it?'

His perspicacity shook her, but she could not resist him.

'I suppose it was,' she admitted. 'Very well, Mr Armitage, I'll do what I can.'

As she went down in the lift she wondered what exactly she had committed herself to doing.

The following day was bright and sunny; Scotland was being kind to them. Ron and George were full of their proposed climb. Jocelyn had told them last night that it really was Dorian Armitage who was staying at the hotel with his son, and that meant explaining about his marriage.

'Always thought the fellow was a dark horse,' was George's comment. 'But I shouldn't think he'd stay here long. It isn't his cup of tea.'

As they sat at breakfast, Dorian came in and paused at their table, evidently waiting to be introduced, while Dorry smiled shyly at Jocelyn.

'I've seen you often enough from the flies,' George said, rising to his feet, 'but I must say I'm surprised to meet you in a place like this, sir. Thought you always went abroad.'

'Exactly, but I visited Scotland when I was a boy, and wanted to see it again.' Dorian turned to Jocelyn. 'Would you like to come with us to Oban while your relations are climbing the Cobbler?'

She had expected she would be asked to take charge of Dorry while his father sought more sophisticated entertainment, not to be included in a joint excursion.

'I ... I'd love too,' she stammered, taken by surprise.

'Good. It's some way, so we'll be starting immediately after breakfast, if that suits you.' He moved on with Dorry in tow.

Ron was delighted by this proposal; he had had some qualms about leaving his sister alone all day. George too had qualms, but for another reason. Dorian Armitage was evidently in search of diversion, the 'getting to know' his son being insufficient for his needs. Long experience of theatre folk had given him a low opinion of their morals, and Dorian was used to easy conquest. But he knew modern youth resented warnings, being confident it could fend for itself. Nevertheless he did venture a mild protest.

'Don't you get too thick with him, Jo. He won't do you any good.'

Jocelyn was aware that her colour had deepened as she said brightly:

'And don't you go getting ideas, Dad. I'm simply going to look after the boy. He ... he's used to female companionship.'

'And so's his lordship,' George jerked his head towards the window table, where Dorian and Dorry were eating their breakfast. 'Only it doesn't stop at companionship.'

At that moment Dorian turned his head and shot them a keen glance. Jocelyn suspected that he knew quite well what the electrician was saying. His fine mouth was curled in sardonic amusement and the eyes that met the girl's had a hint of challenge.

Jocelyn laughed. 'Really, Daddy, after all this time in the theatre I should know how to look after myself! Even if he wanted to, which I'm quite sure he doesn't, Mr Armitage could hardly make a pass at me with the child present.'

George piled marmalade on to a piece of toast. 'A child can be a useful screen for evil intentions,' he muttered.

'Suspicious old thing,' Jocelyn chided him, while Ronald, who did not want to see Jocelyn's day out-vetoed, said with unintentional unkindness:

'Guess he's got far more glamorous fish to fry than poor old Jo.'

As they finished their meal, Dorry, at a nod from his father, came running to their table, his black eyes bright with eagerness.

'*Monsieur, mon père* says it is time we left,' he announced. 'Oh, hurry, *mademoiselle*, he does not like to be kept waiting.'

'Frenchified,' George exclaimed, eyeing the boy doubtfully.

'Yes, I told you about him last night.' Jocelyn realised the information regarding Dorry's French mother had made no impact until the boy opened his lips. 'He speaks both languages.'

Dorian's elegant figure loomed up behind his son. Casually dressed in slacks and pullover, he still contrived to look distinguished. Jocelyn's garb was similar to his, for though it was midsummer, there were plenty of chill breezes to temper the bright sunshine. He asked when she would be ready to start.

'Oh, I'm ready now.' She stood up, picking up her shoulder bag, and met his appraising glance which swept her from crown to toe. She wondered if he had expected her to dress up.

'And we must start too,' Ronald exclaimed. 'We're late as it is.'

'I wish you joy on your trip,' Dorian said lazily. His eyes went to the mountains across the loch. 'It looks tough going to me.'

'Oh, the Cobbler's nothing, it's only two thousand eight hundred and ninety feet, it's the rocks at the top that interest us.'

Dorry asked anxiously: 'There is *vraiment* no man up there, *monsieur*?'

'Mr Seymour,' his father corrected him with a slight frown. 'Do remember to speak English, Dorry.'

'Yes, Papa,' the child said meekly. He slipped his hand into Jocelyn's as if he felt she was a bulwark against Dorian's awe-inspiring presence. 'Come along, *mademoiselle*.'

Dorian's eyebrows went up at the French word and he laughed.

'Incorrigible!'

'He'll soon grow out of it,' Jocelyn told him. 'You can't expect him to change overnight.'

'Ah, but I'm a fast worker myself,' he murmured significantly, as they moved away, and Jocelyn hoped George had not caught that ambiguous remark.

The road went round the top of the loch and through Glen Croe, not to be confused with the much more famous Glencoe. It was a bleak windswept spot, circling the base of the Cobbler. Wild yellow irises grew in profusion wherever there was water among the sparse vegetation while cotton grass nodded in the breeze, but the slopes of the mountain itself were bare and barren ending in naked rock.

Soon Dorian's powerful car was through the glen and the scenery became more genial. Lochs reflected the blue of the sky, trees grew along their shores, the mountains retreated. The Pass of Brander brought them near again, but on its further side the country was more level as the road turned towards the sea.

Jocelyn had insisted upon sitting in the back of the car so that she could give her full attention to her charge. Dorian had raised his brows but accepted her decision. Thus for the most part during their journey she only saw the back of his head and she was careful to sit out of range of the driving mirror. Dorry was soon chattering unrestrainedly in his mixture of French and English without correction from his father. Dorian occasionally mentioned where they were, naming Loch Awe and Loch Etive, but otherwise did not speak.

'You know this country?' she asked, noticing that he drove with confidence and did not refer to a map.

'Yes, as I told your father I spent boyhood holidays here.'

'It's not as pretty as France,' Dorry insisted. 'It's ...' he sought for a word, *'froid,'* he concluded.

'Cold? But it's not cold today, Dorry, and the lochs look beautiful.'

'Dorry's used to vineyards and orchards,' Dorian explained. 'He finds Scotland too austere.'

But the boy was pleased with Oban. The crowds of holidaymakers seemed to stimulate him and the red-funnelled steamers plying to and from the islands excited him, Dorian said to Jocelyn as he skipped ahead of them along the esplanade.

'He seems to be entirely his mother's child. She was a Parisienne and occasionally she had him to stay with her. Those were the high spots in his life, I gather, and his precious Nounou went with him to look after him. Elise insisted she wanted nothing from me, she had means from her parents. I think she feared that if she accepted an allowance from me I might lay claim to Dorry. Though she'd little use for him herself she was determined I shouldn't have him.'

He spoke with bitterness; evidently his wife's action

had wounded him.

'Of course,' he amended, 'an actor and a bachelor can hardly make a home for a child, as she often told me.'

'You weren't divorced?'

'She was a Catholic,' he told her tersely.

Married but without a wife, could Dorian be blamed for the stories that had circulated about him? Jocelyn was intensely aware of his male virility as she walked by his side, and noticed that every woman they passed glanced at him. He would be hardly human if he did not succumb to the flattery and adulation with which he was surrounded, and now at last he was free.

'Jeanne made a great to-do when I went to fetch Dorry, which of course didn't help,' he told her. 'But I couldn't leave him to be raised by Breton peasants. All they could offer him was work in their vineyard.' He lifted his chin arrogantly. 'That's no life for an Armitage, and he is one, though he doesn't look like one.'

'It's early days yet. He may grow more like you, as he gets older,' Jocelyn pointed out, and remembered that Dorry had his father's smile. 'Does he show any signs of dramatic talent?'

'Not yet, but as you say it's early days, but I don't want him to go on the stage, unless he sets his heart upon it.'

'Don't you want him to follow in your footsteps?'

'Exactly, it would be in my footsteps. The son of a well-known actor always has his father's label attached to him. It makes it difficult for him to succeed in his own right. I'll not have Dorry trading on my name.'

This was an unusual attitude to take and she wondered vaguely if he feared a young rival and pushed away the unworthy thought. It would be years before Dorry could emulate his father, if ever.

The object of their discussion came careering back to them.

'Can we go up there?' he demanded, indicating the circle of arches that are such a feature of the Oban landscape and are known as McCaig's Tower.

'If you like, but it's a blot on the scene,' his father returned.

'It's about the most recognisable building in the town,' Jocelyn observed.

'And the least Scottish, except that mercifully it's built of granite.' Dorian turned up a street that connected with George Street, the main thoroughfare, from which a road went up to the tower. It was quite a steep climb.

'It's called McCaig's folly,' he told them, 'because it's only a shell. Work upon it was abandoned when the walls were completed, but its style is more suited to ancient Rome than Scotland.'

'What a lot you know,' Dorry said admiringly.

Dorian winked at Jocelyn. 'There are guide books,' he murmured *sotto voce*.

His description was borne out by the circle of tiered windows like a miniature colosseum enclosing a garden with shrubberies. From the seaward arches Dorian indicated the view over to Mull, which he said was worth the climb.

But Dorry was not interested in views and was disappointed that the Folly did not enclose a castle with dungeons, which its prominent position had led him to suppose.

Dorian suggested lunch and he brightened. For this Dorian selected a restaurant in one of the hotels that fronted the bay. The bay at Oban is practically landlocked, with the Island of Kerrara four miles long across its mouth, thus making half a mile of safe anchorage with entrances to south and north. Although a great tourist centre, Oban is also a fishing port and possesses a tweed mill and a whisky distillery, all being of comparative recent growth, though there had been habitations on the spot since ancient times, albeit there had been nothing more than a cluster of thatched cottages.

Jocelyn was a little dismayed by the course events were taking. She had expected to have sole charge of Dorry, amusing him by paddling in the loch and other childish ploys, instead of which the day was stretching into a lengthy expedition culminating in a meal which would cost Dorian a pretty packet. Nor did he stint her, ordering wine and coffee.

She said in protest: 'I didn't mean to let you treat me, Mr Armitage. I thought I was to take Dorry off your hands.'

'Did I say that?' he enquired, his cat's eyes sparkling. 'Would you condemn me to solitude? I shouldn't find much pleasure in Oban on my own.' He turned to his small son. 'Where would you like to go tomorrow?'

'Could we go on a steamer, Papa?'

'We could get one on Loch Lomond.'

'I want to go on one now,' Dorry insisted, looking out of the window towards a boat which was disembarking passengers at a pier.

'We haven't time, son. We've a long way to go back to Arrochar.'

'We could spend the night here, *mon père*.'

'So we could.' Dorian looked at Jocelyn with an impish grin.

'I must get back,' she said hastily. 'But if you want to stay, I can return by train.'

The West Highland railway ran from Oban to Arrochar.

Dorry's face fell. 'I would not wish to stay without Mademoiselle.'

'In England,' Dorian began patiently, 'young ladies are addressed as Miss and their surname, but perhaps Miss Seymour will allow you to call her by that rather unusual first name of hers, prefixed possibly by Auntie.'

'No, I don't feel like an aunt,' she protested, 'but you can call me Jo.' Aware of Dorian's mocking eyes, she went on quickly: 'It's short for Jocelyn, and it's appropriate because my mother was playing in *Little Women* when ... when she knew I was coming. She was Jo March.'

'You were of course born backstage and cradled in a dress basket,' Dorian purred.

'Nothing of the sort. Mother managed better than that. She gave up acting after I came to make a home for us.'

'What a pity!'

'She wasn't dedicated to it. She found stage life wearing.'

'And are you ... dedicated?'

'Well, I would like to have a bit of success before I retire.'

'Then you are thinking of retiring and making a home for some lucky fellow?'

'Oh no, and there isn't any lucky fellow, as you so gallantly put it.'

He refilled her wineglass. 'When there is,' he persisted, 'will you have to choose between domesticity and your career?'

'It seems rather a remote possibility, but if I married and had a child, I'd put its welfare first, and that wouldn't be promoted by going on tour, as I might have to do.'

Dorian glanced at his small son, who was engrossed in absorbing a large strawberry ice.

'Do I detect criticism in that remark?' he enquired.

'Certainly not. It's different for a man, he's the breadwinner.'

'Indeed? But your notions are a little old-fashioned, aren't they, Jocelyn?'

She started as he again used her name, and looked at him levelly across the intervening table.

'That privilege was meant for Dorry,' she told him coldly.

Golden points of light danced in his green eyes, and he smiled as he returned:

'You told him to call you Jo, which I shall never do. I'm not going to Miss Seymour you, if that's what you mean, and you're quite at liberty to return the compliment.'

'I'd never presume to call you Dorian.'

'Why? Am I such an ogre?'

'It ... it isn't suitable,' she floundered. She knew everybody used first names in the profession, but she wanted to maintain some sort of distance between herself and him. The use of their names evoked an intimacy which she would be better without.

'Of course it's suitable—you really do have archaic notions, Jocelyn, or do you consider I'm so ancient I must be treated with veneration?'

'Yes, but not because of your age, but because of your reputation.'

He sat back and laughed. 'What a double-edged remark! Do you mean deference to my success or a brush-off for my presumption?'

She giggled. 'Both, perhaps.'

'I warn you I'm not easily brushed off. Like the burr, I stick,' he told her nonchalantly, and busied himself lighting a cigar.

'May I blow the match out?' Dorry demanded, finding their conversation unintelligible. This was a ritual when Dorian used matches instead of his lighter. He obligingly held the match towards the boy, who blew lustily, while he observed:

'Be that as it may, Jocelyn you are and Jocelyn you will remain, and I should prefer you to call me Dorian while we are together.'

'Is that an order?'

'Definitely.'

She leaned forward to wipe some ice-cream from Dorry's face with his table napkin.

'Very well, Dorian,' she agreed. 'Do we continue together?'

He said casually: 'For a few days, for Dorry's sake. That was arranged, wasn't it? Later on I may have friends joining me.'

His manner had changed completely, no longer was it semi-flirtatious, and his announcement struck her with an unpleasant chill. Though she had doubts about the wisdom of continuing in close association with him, she did not welcome the prospect of an influx of gay companions who would take him from her. Much better so, she told herself feverishly; he was altogether too attractive, and he did not belong to her sphere. He might find her company entertaining, for a few days, but he would not desire a permanent connection. She checked herself. Permanent connection, indeed, what was she thinking about? This was merely a holiday interlude engineered for Dorry's sake. The cool way in which he had just answered her indicated that though he might condescend to tease her occasionally, he was well aware of the distance between them.

Dorry, replete with ice-cream, gave a long sigh of content and sat back in his chair.

'*Alors, mon père,* if we have no time to go *en bateau,* what do we do now?' he asked.

'I think a little walk before we go back to the car,' his father decreed, 'to shake down that ice.'

Dorry made a moue of disgust. 'I'd like to bathe.'

'Not after that meal. Come, we'll go and look at the Cathedral. That should be uplifting.'

The Cathedral of St Columba, at the north of the esplanade, is built of pink granite. It is small, having a tall tower but no transepts. Dorry, who was used to the lofty churches of France, did not think much of it. They went back to the Corran Park and sat on a seat in the sun watching the tourists' coaches come in and decant their loads in front of the town hall. A little girl with a puppy on a lead came by and Dorry started in pursuit. Soon the two children were engaged in conversation which centred on the puppy. The animal licked Dorry's face, where possibly ice-cream lingered, to his great delight. Then it rolled on its back and both children squatted down to tickle its tummy.

'He begins early,' Dorian said with a chuckle, 'but no Armitage was ever slow with a woman.' He threw Jocelyn an oblique glance.

Ignoring it, she observed coolly: 'He needs the company of other children.'

'He'll get that at school.' Dorian removed his gaze to the bay. 'You're very circumspect, aren't you, Jocelyn?'

'I need to be,' she retorted, wondering if this were the prelude to another flirtatious advance, which she must parry, but it seemed it was not so, for he began to talk about his work.

This holiday was a much needed break after an arduous tour of America, which accounted for the fact that she had seen nothing about him during the winter. Upon his return to London he was to start work upon a historical play in joint management with Aubrey Oliphant, who was lessee of the Paragon Theatre. Both he and Aubrey were enthusiastic about the play, in which he was to star, but it would be something of a gamble.

'We'll probably both lose a packet,' he said wryly, 'but Aubrey thinks it's worth a try. He's making so much with his current musical, he's prepared to take a risk. It centres round John of Gaunt, Duke of Lancaster, and is a mixture of *Richard of Bordeaux* and *Henry VIII*. The first was a triumph for John Gielgud, the latter for Keith Michell. The Henry series centred round each of his six wives—well, John had three. I'd prefer it without the emphasis upon the ladies, but Aubrey insists they're better box office than politics. So it's divided into the three periods. Blanche of Lancaster brought him great wealth, Constanza the Spanish princess the hope of a throne, which he never gained, incidentally, though his daughter became Queen of Castile, but the lead will be Catherine Swynford, who was the love of his life, and whom he eventually married when the others were dead.'

'I suppose Esme Carr will play it?'

'She wants to, though I don't consider she's right for it at all,' Dorian frowned thoughtfully. 'Unfortunately her father has offered to back us fairly substantially, and it will be an expensive production.'

Jocelyn sighed in sympathy, for that was a familiar situation. Actresses acquired leading parts not by virtue of their talent, but because they had influence. Esme would be sure to get the part upon that basis, for though she might not be Dorian's idea of Catherine, she was not incompetent. The love of John Plantagenet's life, and she would endeavour to become that of Dorian's too. Though he had called her insipid, she would have plenty of opportunity to make him change his opinion of her.

She debated whether she dared ask if there would be anything for herself. In this sort of play there would be bound to be a lot of small parts and walk-ons.

'There will be a big cast?' she hinted.

'Enormous, but mostly men. It was a most spectacular period of English history.'

He enlarged upon the pageantry of the Plantagenet court, until he caught her despondent expression and broke off to ask:

'You'd like to be in it?'

'Would there be a chance?'

'Only crowd work, and you're too good for that.'

'I'd take it willingly. I don't suppose there'll be anything better going.'

She looked at him eagerly. Dorian stared down into the smoky blue eyes raised to his, and seemed to be considering. Hope soared—surely he might do this for her?

Dorian turned his head away. 'I'll let you know,' he said offhandedly. Jocelyn looked down at her knees, absurdly disappointed. That empty phrase! He never would let her know, any more than the managers did who used it after an audition. She would have agreed to take anything, however unrewarding, if she could have had the privilege of being in the same production with him. She wondered if she could lower her pride to beg him for a more definite answer, but Dorry had parted from the girl with the puppy and was coming towards them.

'Time we were starting for home,' Dorian said, standing up. 'And we won't talk any more shop while we're on holiday.'

She followed him meekly towards the car, too depressed to venture to protest.

CHAPTER THREE

THEY arrived back at the Highlander before the climbing party put in an appearance. It had become evident to Jocelyn during the homeward drive that Dorian fully intended to make full use of her rash offer to 'help' him with Dorry, a somewhat vague phrase to define unknown duties, and her belated doubts that her father and brother might raise objections, he dismissed with lordly contempt.

'It's your holiday, isn't it? They're doing what they want to do, so why shouldn't you? They ought to be pleased you've found a diversion.'

This observation was accompanied by one of his sly glances, so that she was left wondering if the diversion referred to himself or his son.

But George and Ronald would be only staying another day at Arrochar and might not want to leave her behind with a person whom her father regarded as a dubious character. Nor was she certain that she had definitely promised to take care of Dorry, although Dorian seemed to think she had. She surmised the trip to Oban had been intended as an ante-dated reward for services to come, and that when the friends he had mentioned arrived he would not have much time for the child. Dorry would need her companionship then, and that reflection enabled her to quiet her misgivings and justify a continued stay at Arrochar.

She changed into a long dress of cornflower blue and went down to sit in the vestibule to wait for her family before going in to dinner, where she could amuse herself watching the continual comings and goings.

George and Ronald eventually came in, jubilant after a successful climb, and paused to speak to her on their way to the lift.

'We won't be long,' Ron told her. 'Nice of you to wait for us.'

Dorian and Dorry came towards them from the dining room, having finished their meal, and upon impulse Jocelyn called to Dorry.

'My brother and father have just climbed the Cobbler,' she informed him. 'There's nothing up there at all but some tall pillars of rock.'

Round-eyed, Dorry looked up at the two men, still clad in their anoraks and climbing boots.

'You went up to see? *Messieurs, vous êtes très braves.*'

'Thanks, sonnie, for I imagine that was a compliment,' Ronald said, laughing. 'Did you really believe there was someone there?'.

'My son is too imaginative,' Dorian explained wryly. 'He peoples the world with trolls and fairies, but then his father's an actor, who lives by creating illusions for a gullible public.'

'Such as *The Dream*,' Jocelyn suggested. 'You mayn't credit it, Ron, but we were asked to believe Dorian was the ruler of a magic realm of elves and fairies.'

'Go on!' Ronald ejaculated gaping, for anything less like a denizen of fairyland than Dorian appeared at that moment would be difficult to visualise. He had changed into his dark suit since returning from Oban, and with his immaculate tie and shirt looked more like the hero of an elegant drawing room comedy than a creature of the woods. The hero or the suave villain? His narrow cat's eyes had a wicked glint in them, as he drawled:

'Shakespeare makes Oberon prone to all the human failings, including jealousy, revenge and possessiveness, so I had no difficulty in making him credible.'

'Did you fly?' Dorry asked eagerly, with recollections of such aerobatics in a pantomime he had seen.

'No, son, I was spared that indignity, neither was I supplied with wings.'

'He wore a leopardskin and carried a spear,' Jocelyn described him. 'He looked out of this world.'

'That being in character,' Dorian laughed. 'I was not supposed to be *of* this world, but as this young person very definitely is and has had a long day, I must ask you to excuse us. It's past his bedtime.'

Dorry pulled at Jocelyn's hand. 'You will come and say goodnight when I'm in bed?' he asked anxiously.

'Well, I ...' Jocelyn glanced apologetically at Dorian. It was his room she would be invading.

'A good night kiss is part of your role as comforter,' he told her mockingly. 'But I also am bereaved, don't I qualify for one too?'

'No, you're grown up,' she said hastily. 'Okay, Dorry, I'll come and say goodnight when I've had my dinner.'

The three men and the boy departed for the lift, leaving Jocelyn wishing Dorian had been a little more circumspect in front of her father, who might take his lightly spoken words too seriously.

Ron and George soon returned, having made a quick toilet, and over dinner, Ron told her that they had decided to go on to Fort William next day as there was no other mountain in the Loch Long area that attracted them.

'But you seem to have got yourself a commitment,' he observed, 'so perhaps you'll want to stay on here? We don't mind if you find that small boy an attraction. I know you like children, but you don't need a holiday task, surely?'

'I don't regard it as a task,' she returned, 'and it's very pleasant here. I'd much prefer it to a town, which I understand Fort William is.'

George was looking doubtful, as she had feared. He had, as she had also feared, noted the easy familiarity between her and the actor, and that she had addressed him by his first name. He knew they had been in the same production some while back, which constituted a link, but it was a link he would prefer to see broken.

'I think you'd be wiser to leave with us tomorrow,' he said bluntly.

'Daddy, I can't. The child is beginning to lean on me,' she protested. 'He's got a difficult transition to make to fit him for a changed environment, and I believe I can help him. I want to help him.'

George's blue eyes, so like her own, looked straight into hers.

'Are you sure it's because of the boy, or is it on his father's account that you want to stay here?'

Jocelyn dropped her eyes. 'The child, of course,' she insisted. 'Mr Armitage is expecting friends to join him shortly and I'm afraid poor little Dorry will feel neglected unless I'm here.'

Ronald laughed. 'Have a heart, Dad. If Jo wants to make the running with this famous heart-throb why must you come the heavy father?'

Jocelyn flashed an indignant glance at him. 'The last thing I want to do is make the running with Do . . . Mr Armitage.'

'No?' Ron grinned sceptically. 'I don't blame you, Jo. Have fun if you can.'

'I don't want Jo to get hurt,' George explained. 'I don't trust young Armitage. I know too much about him.'

'You don't, you're judging him by theatre gossip,' Jocelyn reproved him. 'After all, I've been over two years on the stage and I know how to deal with wolves. Not that Mr Armitage is a wolf,' she amended hastily, 'but you know how free and easy professional manners are. I assure you we're both only thinking of the child.'

She emphasised her last sentence, for naturally it was only because of Dorry that she wanted to stay in Arrochar, and Dorian wanted her to remain, but even as she spoke, she seemed to see the glint of green-gold eyes deriding her assertion.

'Right, you do as you please, Jo,' George agreed. 'But if you change your mind you can get a train to Fort William and come to join us. We'll be pleased to welcome you.'

'When we come down from our mountain peaks,' Ronald supplemented. 'Actually, I'm very glad you've found some friends and we don't have to feel guilty about leaving you alone.'

As promised, Jocelyn went up to Dorian's room after she had finished her meal. Not wanting to encounter Dorian upstairs, she glanced into the bar to ascertain if he were downstairs and glimpsed him exchanging repartee with Ronald's barmaid.

Mrs McTavish and a friend, en route for the upstairs lounge, came up in the lift with her, and glanced at her curiously as she entered Dorian's room.

Dorry was wide awake and clung to her a little nervously. He looked very small and lonely in the emptiness of the double room.

'I shan't be far away,' she told him. 'I'm going to sit in the sun lounge, which is next door, and I won't shut you in so I can hear you if you call out, but you must try to go to sleep.'

He seemed satisfied and snuggled down in his bed. As promised she wedged the door slightly ajar and went into the lounge. As she came through the connecting glass door she saw Mrs McTavish look at her friend with raised brows, and she had an impulse to go to them and explain about Dorry, but decided it was making too much out of nothing and it was not their business if she chose to befriend Dorian's child.

The next day was again bright and sunny. George

and Ronald had made an early start, and she went in to a solitary breakfast after seeing them off, for she had not been down in time to have it with them.

George said: 'Be good,' and Ronald, 'Be careful,' and then they were gone.

The Armitages were seated at their window table as she entered the dining room, and seeing she was alone, Dorian spoke to the waiter, then came across to her.

'I've told him to lay your place at our table. You'll join us, of course.'

Remembering the inquisitive glances she had earned last night in the lounge, she returned:

'That's very kind of you, Mr Armitage, but I don't mind sitting alone, and it's better ...'

'Better for whom?' he interrupted. 'Don't be absurd. Come along.'

He took hold of her arm and short of making a scene she could not resist him. She sat down as the waiter placed a chair for her and said with vexation:

'You're a bit high-handed, Mr Armitage.'

'Naturally, have you forgotten I'm a king? I thought I asked you to use my name.'

Dorry said anxiously: 'You're not cross, Mademoiselle Jo? Didn't you want to sit with me?'

Jocelyn laughed ruefully. 'I'm not cross, darling, and of course I like sitting with you ...' she shot a barbed glance at Dorian, 'I don't like being ordered about. Your father forgets that I'm no longer a child too.'

'I assure you I've never considered you are a child,' Dorian told her, with the familiar glint in his eyes. The sunlight illuminated the smooth brown planes of his face, and a little mocking smile twisted his well-cut lips. He was looking intensely attractive, and remembering her father's warning, Jocelyn began to wonder if she had been very rash; she had not anticipated being asked to join him for meals. As if sensing her doubt he told her: 'I couldn't let you sit all alone among a crowd of strangers. That wouldn't be friendly.'

'You're very considerate.' She had no cause for alarm, yet instinct was warning her there was an ulterior motive behind his courtesy.

The waiter brought her eggs and bacon and fresh coffee. Dorry was chattering about their previous day's outing and she responded absently, aware Dorian was watching her closely, and without speaking. Tension seemed to be growing between them and she could not meet his eyes.

As she finished her meal, she said with an effort:

'Well now, Mr Armitage, if you'd like a day off, I'll take Dorry for a steamer trip on Loch Lomond.'

'And how will you get there? It's nearly two miles.'

'There'll be a bus or a train to Tarbet.'

'What's wrong with my car?'

'I didn't want to bother you, so you can have a free day.'

His black brows rose in mock disapproval. 'Really, Miss Seymour, you speak as if my poor little boy was an imposition I'm trying to avoid. Didn't I explain that we're getting to know each other? Now you want to take him away from me, refusing to let me drive you to the lake. Aren't you being rather heartless?'

Bewildered, she exclaimed: 'But I thought...' She checked herself, seeing Dorry's puzzled expression. 'I thought you wanted me to look after him.'

'To the exclusion of myself? Can't you look after me too?'

'You're a grown man.'

'I can't help that, and grown men also suffer from loneliness. Any reason why you shouldn't be my companion as well as Dorry's?'

'Yes, a whole lot of reasons.'

'Such as?'

'I can't explain in front of the child.'

'Are they so shocking?'

'Oh, really Dorian!' she exclaimed with exasperation. 'I should have thought they were obvious.'

He smiled with satisfaction. 'There, you've been provoked into using my name. That's how you really think of me, isn't it?'

She was about to deny this, but Dorry, who had been unable to follow their conversation, broke in impatiently.

'Why we sitting here, Papa? It's lovely outside, and you talk and talk.'

Dorian looked at him solemnly.

'I'm trying to persuade Jocelyn to allow me to accompany you on your steamer trip. She wants to leave me behind.'

Dorry looked from one to the other.

'Aren't you both coming?' he asked anxiously.

'That's for her to say.'

'Oh, you're being absurd!' Jocelyn cried with annoyance at the way he had twisted her offer to suit some devious purpose of his own. 'I never meant to imply that you weren't wanted, only...'

'But we do want him, don't we Mademoiselle Jo?' Dorry broke in. 'It wouldn't be kind to leave him behind.'

'And Jocelyn's such a kind person,' Dorian purred.

'Oh, you!' She rose to her feet. 'Shall we go?' she enquired coldly.

With Dorry unconsciously abetting his father she had no option, and she was secretly elated that Dorian did not intend to stay behind, and another enchanted day lay before them.

Nor on the succeeding days did he listen to her protests, and she soon ceased to make them. Scotland was generous to them, presenting them with a sequence of lovely weather. The Loch Lomond expedition was followed by a trip to the Trossachs, another to the Bridge of Orchy, and Dorian expounded about Rob Roy and the Lady of the Lake, for it was MacGregor country, and Scott had chosen it for the background to his poem. Dorian gave them lunches at the best places available and Jocelyn sat at his table in the hotel dining room for breakfast and dinner. In the evenings he waited while she put Dorry to bed and then insisted upon giving her coffee in the lounge or a drink in the bar. On these occasions he told her more about the Plantagenet play with great enthusiasm. His manner throughout was exemplary, he might have been her brother, except for the expression in his strange eyes when he looked at her, an expression she could not interpret, except that it made her uneasy. The other visitors in the hotel obviously considered they were a family. More than once a friendly woman spoke to her about 'your little boy', but Jocelyn did not correct her; there was no need to go into long explanations with a passing acquaintance. That Dorian overheard and favoured her with that derisive smile of his did not embarrass her, as she suspected he hoped it might; the mistake was too trivial to trouble her. Dorian seemed to delight in pushing her into equivocal situations, but he made no attempt to take advantage of them. She concluded that he was merely satisfying his sardonic sense of humour.

The friends he had mentioned did not arrive, and Jocelyn was content to allow him to continue to organise their holiday. She was gratified that he seemed to find pleasure in her company, as he must do, since he made no effort to avoid her. As for Dorry, he openly adored her, finding her more than an adequate substitute for his lost Nounou. About that Jo felt some qualms of conscience. It was hardly fair to encourage him to become attached to her when inevitably she must leave him. But their association need not be severed entirely, for eventually they would all be returning to London, and unless Dorian was utterly heartless, he would not forbid her access to the child, so she could continue to see him. She was well aware that Dorry would at the same time present a link with his father, and though Dorian would be absorbed in his new production she might occasionally encounter him; nor had she given up hope that she might be able to obtain a small part in the play, in spite of his lack of response to her hint.

For if she were honest she would have had to admit that fond as she was of Dorian's son, it was Dorian himself who was the main attraction. She knew it was hopeless to fall in love with him, but she could not help herself. He had become the focus of her romantic yearnings when she had first seen him in *The Dream*, and contact with him had done nothing to disillusion her. Now she had met him on an equal footing, Dorian the man was even more intriguing than the actor had been, and since fate had given her a succession of enchanted days, she resolutely ignored the painful future to bask in the sunlit present.

It could not last. She was, as she was dimly aware, playing with fire. Dorian was not a man who could associate daily with an attractive young woman and be content to permit the situation to remain static. Used to feminine adulation, he did not believe in her assumption of indifference; he had but to hold out his arms and she would fall into them.

There were places along Loch Lomond reserved as picnic areas, but these always had their quota of visitors of whom Dorian did not approve. A long strip of the western bank enclosed the estate of Rossdhu House and he had obtained permission to enjoy its private precints where visitors to the house were not allowed. They went there one afternoon of midsummer sunshine, taking a picnic pasket, for Dorry had developed a passion for al fresco meals, and his father had bought the necessary equipment.

The Loch, mirroring the cloudless sky, was azure blue as it is shown on picture postcards but so often is not in reality. A dense copse of rhododendrons in full colour—they bloom late in Scotland—screened them from observation. Their meal eaten, they lay on the turf beside the margin of the loch, and Dorry, exhausted by his activities of the pre-tea hours, fell asleep. His father remarked that he would be prey to the midges which frequented the water's edge as evening approached and carried him to the car, lying him full length on the back seat.

'Too many late nights,' he observed. 'You should send him to bed earlier.'

Jocelyn paused in her work of repacking the picnic basket and looked up at him indignantly.

'I like that!' she exclaimed. 'It's you who always gives in to him when he asks if he can stay up a few minutes longer. Besides, it's light so late now it's rather hard to have to go to bed while the sun's still shining.'

Dorian was contemplating his sleeping son through the car window. He moved away and sat down by Jocelyn, who hurriedly resumed her task.

'I said he was spoilt in France, but I'm afraid you and I are continuing the treatment.'

'I suppose neither of us are disciplinarians,' she suggested. 'After all, it's holiday time. Are you really going to send him to boarding school? Isn't he rather young?'

'What else can I do? I shall be working day and night, and a bachelor's flat is hardly suitable for a young child.'

'You could get a housekeeper.'

'They're not always reliable. I manage with a domestic help.' He shifted his position in an attempt to see Jocelyn's face. 'Perhaps a mistress would be a better proposition.'

Inadvertently she caught his glance. He was looking at her with a wicked gleam in his eyes, and she hurriedly looked away, pushing the plastic plates so hard into the basket that she jammed her thumb.

'Damn!' she exclaimed, sucking it, but the incident gave her time to recover her self-possession, and she went on coolly: 'I don't think that would be a good idea at all. You want someone who'll devote herself to the boy, not be absorbed in you.'

'She could perhaps do both, as you've been doing.'

'But I'm not absorbed in you,' she declared vehemently. 'You know I only stayed on here because of Dorry.'

'Did you, my dear?'

Eyes and mouth were mocking. His short-sleeved shirt was open at the neck, which like his smooth arms was burned a rich tan by the sun; his regular features were etched against the dark bushes behind him. Except for his dark hair, he was again Oberon, King of the fairy realm, and the setting could have been that enchanted wood near Athens, but Jocelyn was hardly Titania, that dainty, ethereal being, for her burnished hair was windswept and tangled, her tank top and trews utilitarian, not diaphanous drapery. She sat back on heels and regarded him severely.

'Yes,' she said firmly. 'But for him I'd be at Fort William with Ron and Dad.'

'Come off it, girl. That was the excuse you gave them, but it didn't deceive me.'

'I don't know what you mean, Mr Armitage.'

'Don't be thick.' He reached for her, taking hold of her upper arms, and drew her towards him. 'You know what I mean. Good lord, I've been nearly a week in your company and I haven't kissed you yet.'

Jocelyn was wise enough to know that resistance would only excite him, so she made no attempt to avoid the very ardent kiss he pressed upon her mouth, but her lips were firmly closed under his.

Holding her close against him, he drew back his head and looked into her pale face, whence all the colour had fled. 'What's the matter? I expected a better response than that.'

Reluctantly she disengaged herself, and he did not try to stay her. Her heart was beating so hard she thought he must hear its tumult. With every nerve in her body she longed to yield to him, but she would not so cheapen herself. She saw in a flash that he had deliberately engineered this situation, expecting her to accept him when he was ready to claim her, but he only regarded her as a passing diversion.

'To avoid any further misunderstandings, I'll say here and now that I'm not available,' she told him with a calmness she did not feel.

'To me . . . or to anybody?'

'To nobody.'

'Untouched by passion's fitful fires,' he said ruminatively. He did not seem to be angered by her rejection, he was merely amused. 'How old are you, Jocelyn?'

'Twenty-two.'

'And how long have you been on the stage?'

'Coming up for three years.'

'And you expect me to believe that you lack experience?'

She pulled absently at the grass beside her and was silent.

'Good lord, my colleagues must have been a bit slow, or are you an ice maiden?'

'Nothing so poetic.' She stared at the handful of grass she had plucked. She could not tell him that his image had obsessed her for so long that no other man had been able to arouse any emotion in her. 'Guess I've just been too interested in my job to bother about boys.'

'Ah, your job. You aspire to be an actress? But how can you advance beyond stupid ingenues without a knowledge of life?'

'Is amorous adventure necessary to become a competent actress?'

'Definitely. How can you portray passion, loss and despair if you haven't experienced them?'

Jocelyn thought she was likely to encounter the last two in the near future if not fulfilment of the first, but she returned with spirit:

'The logical conclusion to be drawn from that argument is that I couldn't play Lady Macbeth convincingly unless I'd committed a murder.'

'You've a quick tongue, Jocelyn.' He was lying full length on the grass, and he raised himself on one elbow to regard her quizzically. 'That is rather an extreme case, but what I mean is, you're unawakened. Until you realise your womanhood you won't be a great actress.'

She resumed her absent plucking of the turf beside her, wishing he would look away from her. His intent gaze had a mesmeric quality, and she was suspicious of whence this catechism was leading.

'Oh, I expect I'll fall in love some time,' she said vaguely.

He laughed. 'Why not start by falling for me?' he asked coaxingly. 'Lots of women have, and without any encouragement.' He paused, and Jocelyn turned her head away. The blue water of the loch shimmered before her unseeing eyes. She had no wish to add her name to the list of Dorian's conquests.

'There's no time like the present,' he went on, his voice soft and wheedling. 'You're missing a heaven-sent opportunity. In this day and age you can't have moral scruples. Are you being coy, or shy?'

She raised her eyes to his and told him: 'Neither, and I suppose I should be flattered that the great

Dorian Armitage is prepared to educate me, but I admire him too sincerely to allow him to so cheapen himself.'

His eyelids flickered and he reddened, but almost instantly he recovered his aplomb.

'So you think an affair with you would cheapen me? I wonder why. We shouldn't be doing anyone any harm.'

'Only ourselves. As you say, I haven't had much emotional experience, but affairs, however ephemeral and harmless, must detract from what should be a profound feeling. I mean, if you have a gold nugget, and keep chipping pieces off it, it lessens the value of the gold, which you might one day want to give in its entirety.'

Dorian was quick enough to follow her somewhat involved metaphor.

'Your gold of course being love?'

'Yes.' A delicate colour flooded her face. 'I prefer to keep mine intact until...' her voice died away; she had been going to say until she met the man who would appreciate it, but she had already bestowed her love where it would not be valued.

'Some poor man is going to have a bit of a load to carry.' Dorian said contemptuously.

She shrank inwardly at his tone; so he would find love a burden, he would have no use for a sincere and faithful emotion, he would consider it a tie that would curtail his freedom. A possible explanation of this attitude occurred to her.

'You've become cynical because you've lost your wife—I mean—' She faltered as he frowned. 'Didn't you love her once?'

'And learned my lesson,' he said harshly. 'That was over in less than two years. We shouldn't have married.'

He turned away from her, stretching himself on the

grass, and stared up through the branches of the trees to the sky above him. 'Your trouble, my girl, is that you expect too much from life. Few of us experience great loves or great hates outside the realm of drama, which exaggerates them. Existence is a comedy, not a tragedy. You'd enjoy it much more if you took what came along, like I do.'

'That sounds horribly mediocre.'

'Life is mediocre for most of us, but it can be quite amusing.'

He closed his eyes, and Jocelyn studied him wistfully. She did not want the light ephemeral affair he had offered her, a piquante sauce to round off a holiday, but she might not have held back if he had shown signs of any genuine feeling for her. That might have ripened into something worth while, but she could not pretend that he saw in her anything more than a means to while away an idle hour. If she was crazy enough to yield to him, he would play with her and drop her when he was tired of the game or it became expedient to do so.

A bee buzzed by in the simmering afternoon heat. Jocelyn thought Dorian had fallen asleep, until he said drowsily:

'In *The Dream*, you'll remember the plot turned on the juice of a flower which when squeezed upon a sleeper's eyelids caused him—or her—to fall madly in love with the first object seen upon awakening.'

'So what?'

'I was wondering if there really was such a herb. Do you think the foxgloves of which we see so many about here might do the trick?'

'I'm quite sure they wouldn't. Foxgloves produce digitalis, which is a poison.'

'But it's also a heart stimulant, so it might work.'

'The "little western flower" was certainly not a foxglove,' she said decisively. 'But since you jeer at true love why are you interested in a charm to evoke it?'

He sat up abruptly and said vehemently:

'I'd like to see you wildly and hopelessly in love, my little icicle.'

Keep it cool, her instinct warned her, and she returned lightly:

'Even if "some vile thing was near"?' quoting from the play. 'You were a bit merciless to poor Titania.'

'Served her right,' he said offhandedly. His lids drooped, his lashes veiling the glitter in his eyes. 'It's your reactions in the throes of passion that would be ... so entertaining.'

'Oh, really!' She turned her shoulder towards him. She was in love, hopelessly if not madly, but she would not give him the amusement he desired. She suspected the preamble about the magic flower had been an attempt to lead her into self-betrayal. 'I think Dorry is waking up,' she told him, noticing convulsive movements in the back of the car, and scrambled to her feet. Picking up the picnic basket, she asked:

'Are we moving on, or does Your Majesty intend to lie there in the hope that Puck or some such will come along and put a spell on you?'

He sprang to his feet with a quick lithe movement, laughing gaily.

'The sylvan scene must have bewitched me, but thanks to your cool common sense the magic has flown.' He strode over to the car. 'Hi, infant, feeling better for your snooze? It's time we made a move, I'm bored with this place.'

Quite time, Jocelyn thought as she followed with the basket. That was all it had been, an attempt to enliven the afternoon by flirting with her, and since she had refused to give him the amusement he had anticipated, he was bored. Nor did he seem disappointed by her rebuttal. It showed how shallow were his feelings towards her and emphasised anew how lightly he regarded matters of the heart.

She put her burden into the boot and closed it. Dorian was leaning against the open doorway of the car, gently teasing the child, but Dorry was looking round for her.

'Come and sit with me, Mademoiselle Jo,' he begged, for he could not bring himself to address her without a title, and his literal mind refused the pseudo one of 'Auntie.'

'But she isn't *ma tante,*' he had objected.

'Of course, darling,' she acceded, and Dorian stood aside to let her get in.

Standing with his hands in his pockets, his eyes on the loch, he remarked casually:

'My grandmother phoned to say she's arriving tomorrow. She's anxious to meet my son, whom she hasn't seen for a long while.'

'Your grandmother?' she was surprised. 'You told me you were expecting friends.'

'My grandmother is my best friend,' he announced cryptically. 'But I didn't expect she would venture alone. I'm delighted that she has.' He swung round and looked at Jocelyn with narrowed eyes. 'I hope you won't monopolise Dorry while she's here.'

'I've never tried to monopolise him,' she cried, stung by this unjust implication. 'I'll arrange to leave for Fort William by the first train in the morning.'

She felt a sudden constriction round her heart. She had not expected such an abrupt termination to her stay. Dorian must be annoyed by her rejection after all and was summarily dismissing her.

Dorry gave a wail.

'*Non,* Mademoiselle Jo, *ne vas pas. Ma grandmère, elle est effroyable!*' In his agitation he relapsed into French. '*J'ai peur!*'

'Idiot,' said his father tersely. 'She's not frightful at all, though she is a trifle intimidating.' He glanced enigmatically at Jocelyn. 'Surely, Miss Seymour, you aren't going to throw your protégé to the lions? He'll need your support.'

'You've just told me you didn't want me to monopolise him—there was only one construction I could put upon that.'

'Was there?' He favoured her with his most charming smile. 'I only meant she might misinterpret your motives if you seemed too possessive, but please don't run away.'

Jocelyn was puzzled. She was almost certain that he had wanted her to go, and had chosen a rather oblique way of telling her so, but now he seemed to have changed his mind, presumably because Dorry had been so upset.

'I think you'll get on with my grandmother,' he went on sunnily, 'and she might be able to help you.'

'In what way?'

'Dame Eleanor has a lot of influence.'

Jo had almost forgotten the theatrical connotation.

'Is that a bribe?' she asked doubtfully.

Dorry pulled at her hand, his eyes big with anxiety.

'Don't go, Mademoiselle Jo, please!'

She wavered, unable to withstand his pleading look.

'Perhaps not tomorrow,' she conceded. 'I'll wait and see how you get on, but I'll have to go some time.'

'Why?' Dorian demanded.

She stared at his inscrutable face.

'My position isn't permanent."

'It could be, if you became my housekeeper,' he said blandly.

'You know that's impossible,' she said firmly.

He raised his brows. 'With no strings attached?'

'There'd be gossip,' she began feebly.

He shrugged his shoulders. 'I never bother about that. Would you consider it?'

'No, I'm an actress and not domesticated,' she returned.

If he were serious, he was offering her a seemingly respectable situation under cover of which he would expect to get his own way, she would not consider it for one moment.

'Ah, the career,' he observed, 'but my flat has open doors right on to the stage.'

'Maybe, but I'm not that sort of girl, Dorian.' Aware that Dorry was looking at her eagerly, she added reproachfully: 'It's not fair to the boy to raise his hopes when you're not serious.'

'I'm perfectly serious.'

She braced herself as she realised that she had underestimated him. Far from being put off by her rejection, he had returned to the attack and was quite unscrupulous. Not only was he using Dorry but her hopes of a career to press home his advantage.

'There could only be one outcome if I agreed,' she told him in a low tense voice, 'and that makes it impossible.'

'Not necessarily,' he returned. 'I don't force my attentions upon any woman, you needn't fear for your virtue.'

Did he suspect that it was not his attentions that she feared but her own wayward heart? Had she betrayed herself by her insistence upon the inevitable outcome? His successes had made him supremely confident, and he knew he had only to stay passive and she would come to him in time.

Naturally Dorry had not understood what they were talking about, but he had his own solution of the problem.

'If you married Mademoiselle Jo, Papa, she would be my *maman*,' he announced. 'Then she would stay with me always.'

'There's no guarantee of that,' Dorian said bitterly,

and went to get into the driver's seat.

'What does he mean?' Dorry asked Jocelyn.

'I . . . I don't know,' she told him, but she understood very well. She could not explain to the child that Elise had deserted her husband, and to a lesser degree himself. But Elise's conduct accounted for her husband's cynicism. He preferred liaisons to marriage because she had let him down, and even for his son's sake he would not risk marrying again.

'But cheer up, little one,' she went on brightly. 'I'm still here for the present, and perhaps you'll like your granny, your great-granny, so much you won't miss me. After all, I'm no relation.'

'I wish you were,' Dorry said sadly.

Jocelyn knew that the consolation she had offered was somewhat feeble, and Dorian's derisive laugh from the front seat indicated that he agreed with her.

CHAPTER FOUR

THE next day was wet. Mist covered the Cobbler and its surrounding mountains. Jocelyn sat with Dorry in the lounge, playing childish games—Snap, Beggar my Neighbour and Old Maid, with a borrowed pack of cards. Dorian had gone down to Glasgow to meet Dame Eleanor, who had come up by train. They had decided that the long drive would be tedious for the child and he would be happier with Jocelyn.

'Since I've stayed for his sake it's up to me to do what I can for him,' she had remarked.

Dorian had made no rejoinder, merely gave her one of his enigmatical looks and went out to his car.

Dorry and Jocelyn had lunch together in the hotel dining room and as time passed, the boy became more and more gloomy. She divined that he was apprehensive about meeting the old lady, whom he visualised as a sort of dragon—an illusion Jocelyn found difficult to dispel, for Dame Eleanor Mainwaring had the reputation of being something of a dragon in the profession. She could not imagine her in the role of cosy grandmother. Yet Dorian seemed to be fond of her, so she must have a softer side which she would show to her timid little great-grandson.

In the afternoon the weather cleared and Jo was able to take Dorry for a walk along the loch side. The mist rolled up the sides of the mountains and their summits came into view. Dorry looked up at the crest of the Cobbler.

'If I'd a gun I'd shoot him,' he announced. 'Bang! Bang!'

'You silly boy, there isn't anything to shoot. Ron told you there's only a mass of rocks.'

Dorry shook his head.

'There is a man there, and he's *méchant*—bad.' He gave her a sly look. 'I've got too much 'magination,' he declared importantly.

He had heard his father say that, and Jocelyn quailed as she recalled other indiscreet remarks that had been made in his hearing. She hoped fervently that he would not come out with them in front of his great-grandmother, especially if he had misinterpreted them. Dorian would be no help in such an impasse; he took a perverse pleasure in her embarrassment. However, she would be expected to take a back seat when the actress arrived, and she must expect to be ignored. Such indifference would be a little painful after the easy intimacy she had enjoyed with Dorian during the pask week, but that could not continue, must not continue; it was too dangerous. As for his suggestion that she should function as his housekeeper-cum-Dorry's nannie, that could not even be contemplated seriously. Dorian's flat was taboo. She could not, would not become his mistress, which must be his real intention.

So her thoughts went back and forth, while she answered Dorry's barrage of questions. Loch Long was actually an arm of the sea, and brown fronds of seaweed were discernible in its waters. There was the usual cloud of seagulls and other varieties of waterfowl. Fauna and flora gave Dorry food for conjecture and many of his questions she found unanswerable. He had an enquiring mind. Why was seaweed brown and gulls white? Protective colouring, she suggested. But the gulls were conspicuous against the dark mountainside.

'They're out of their element,' she told him.

'Why?'

He had brought a bag of stale bread cajoled out of the waiters and as the birds swooped and screamed after his bounty, she thought of a plausible answer:

'They come here because you give them scraps.'

'But they didn't know I was going to give them bread.'

'They've learned that most people do.'

'How do they know anybody's going to feed them?'

'Dorry, I'm not an expert on seagull psychology,' she said wearily, to be countered with:

'What's psycho . . . what you said?'

So it went on.

They found a cottage that did teas and after that they returned to the hotel as it started to rain again. Dorry was splashed with mud and needed a wash and a change. Jocelyn went up with him to his room, which was also Dorian's room, and perforce had to assist with his toilet. She could not let his father return to be confronted by muddy pants and shoes in the middle of the floor, which was where Dorry deposited them, but she could never enter the bedroom without a sense of trespass.

She left Dorry in the sun lounge gazing disconsolately out at the rain falling into the loch while she changed her own clothes. She put on the long blue dress which was so becoming to her. It had a square neckline and she did her hair in two coiled plaits, one over each ear. The effect was definitely mediaeval and it occurred to her that she had unconsciously sought to identify herself with Dorian's Plantagenet play. It would do no harm, she thought wryly, to remind him that she was an actress needing an engagement. Then she recalled that he had hinted that he might help her at a price, and her garb might be taken to indicate that she was weakening. There was no time to change as she had left Dorry quite long enough to his own devices, and the odds were that Dorian would not notice her appearance.

Dorry was chatting amiably with Mrs McTavish, and as Jocelyn approached, she said with her twittery manner:

'What a bright little lad your son is. I've so enjoyed our conversation. He tells me your husband's gone to fetch his granny from Glasgow and he doesn't remember ever seeing her. She'll be thrilled to meet him again. If he were mine I'd dote on him.'

Jocelyn felt her colour rise, but she said composedly:

'They'll be here any minute now. Come along, Dorry, we'll go down to meet them?

Dorry gave a little bow to his companion, a trick he had learned in France, which delighted the Scotswoman.

'*Au revoir, madame,*' he said politely. 'But Mademoiselle Jo isn't my *maman.* My *Papa* wants her to come and live with us in London, and so do I, but she said there'd be ... What was it, Mademoiselle Jo? Ah, I remember, gossip. What does that mean, *madame*?'

Madame was staring at Jocelyn with icy disapproval.

'Something laddies shouldn't know anything about,' she said severely. 'You better run along now.'

As they moved away, Jocelyn heard her mutter. 'Such permissive ways are a disgrace!'

There goes my reputation, Jocelyn thought as they went down in the lift, while Dorry asked anxiously:

'Did I make the *gaffe*?'

'No, dear, of course not.'

He sighed: 'I wish you were my *maman.* Then you wouldn't ever go away.'

Jocelyn silently echoed his wish.

Dame Eleanor was standing at the reception desk as Jocelyn and Dorry came out of the lift. She was unmistakable. Her fine aquiline nose, dark piercing eyes that age had not dimmed and regal carriage were familiar to Jocelyn from seeing her in many stage and television appearances. A red velvet cap covered her white curls, and a dark red cloak swung from her angular shoulders. Dorian was standing behind her as she signed the register, and beside him was another familiar figure. Jocelyn experienced a slight shock, for Dorian had said nothing to prepare her for this arrival. The gilded hair and round blue eyes were well known to her—Esme Carr, Titania, small, dainty, dressed more suitably for a fashion parade than the Scottish Highlands in a perfectly tailored two-piece, her tiny feet encased in high-heeled flimsy shoes that would trip her up on any mountain road. Jocelyn wondered vaguely what could have brought Esme to Loch Long where she was so obviosuly out of her element.

Dorian caught sight of them and nudged his grandmother.

'Gran, here is Dorry.'

The august lady swung round and held up old-fashioned lorgnettes—an affectation, for she could see perfectly well without them, and Dorry shrank against Jocelyn, his fingers clutching her skirt. The silent scrutiny took in every detail of the child's appearance, and also Jocelyn's.

'Say hello to your grandmother,' Dorian prompted.

Dorry's proclivity for exactitude overcame his shyness.

'She's my great-grandmother,' he declared, and as Jocelyn gave him a gentle push, he advanced a step and made his French bow.

'*Comment allez-vous, madame?*' As always when disturbed he relapsed into French.

'Obviously Elise's child,' Dame Eleanor said. Her voice was still deep and resonant. She held out her hand. 'Come to me, *mon petit*, I won't eat you.' She smiled, and her smile was singularly sweet.

It reassured Dorry, who went to her and took the extended hand.

'Introduce me to your beautiful friend,' the old woman went on, looking over the boy's head towards Jocelyn. 'She's the lady your father says has been so kind to you, isn't she?'

'Jocelyn Seymour,' Dorian spoke for his son. 'Jocelyn, have you met Dame Eleanor?'

Jocelyn said she had not had that honour, though she had often seen her and admired her work.

'Zut!' Dame Eleanor snapped her fingers. 'Don't flatter an old woman, my dear. I'm well past my prime, but you're approaching yours.'

Esme Carr, who had been watching this exchange with a little supercilious smile, now intervened.

'She's still a long way to go,' she announced. 'I remember you, Jocelyn, you were one of my attendants in *The Dream*. Done anything since?'

'A season in provincial rep.'

'How unutterably grim! I can never bear to leave London, but of course you can't afford to be choosey.' She turned to Dorian. 'Dor, darling, could we have dinner before I go to my room? I'm simply famished.'

'Dinner is being served now,' the receptionist told them, as she handed them their keys.

'Well, come along.' Esme linked her arm through Dorian's, but he hung back.

'What about you, Gran?'

'Oh, I'll join you.'

He disengaged himself from Esme and put a guiding hand under Dame Eleanor's elbow.

'The dining room is up those steps on the left.'

'You'd better go with them,' Jocelyn said to Dorry.

'Aren't you coming?'

'Presently.'

But he would not budge without her and the others seemed to have forgotten him. Somewhat reluctantly she joined the little procession into the dining room. Their usual table in the window was not large enough for the increased party, and a waiter was showing Dame Eleanor to a centre one. Jocelyn pushed Dorry towards it, and retreated to the entrance, meaning to ask for a single for herself. Dorian was settling Dame Eleanor in a chair, handing her cloak to an obsequious waiter; the hotel staff were fully aware that this was a V.I.P. Dorry remained standing, looking towards her, and demanded shrilly:

'Where's Mademoiselle Jo sitting?'

'Does it matter?' Esme asked insolently. 'This table's only laid for four. I hate being cramped.'

Dorian glanced at it. 'Nonsense, there's heaps of room. Waiter, set another place.' He strode towards Jocelyn. 'What's this? You don't have to exile yourself.'

'I'll be intruding,' she murmured.

'It's not you who are intruding,' he returned. 'I'd no idea Esme was coming. It seems she latched on to Gran when she discovered she was coming to join me and insisted that Gran wasn't up to travelling alone, which didn't please Gran at all.'

He laid a masterful hand upon her arm as Jocelyn still hung back.

'You must come and support Dorry,' he said coaxingly. 'He finds the *grande dame* act a little overwhelming.' And true enough, the boy was gazing at her entreatingly.

Somewhat unwillingly Jocelyn allowed herself to be overruled and found herself sitting between Dame Eleanor and Dorry, who heaved a sigh of relief as she took her place. His father was on his other side and Esme next to him. Conversation centred upon their journey and the weather which had greeted them so sourly.

'We've had some lovely days,' Dorian told them. 'Too bad it's broken just when you've arrived.'

'It'll pick up again,' Dame Eleanor said optimistically. 'The forecast is good. How's the play going, Dorian? I hear it's scheduled for the autumn.'

'With any luck, but the musical at the Paragon is still drawing full houses. Aubrey is so keen he threatens to take it off to make room for the play, but we'll be trying it out in the provinces first, it all rather depends upon how they receive it.'

'It's cast?' Esme asked negligently.

'Not completely, one or two parts are still presenting difficulties. We can't get the people we want, they aren't available.'

'I shouldn't think it mattered, because you'll be the only one that counts,' Esme declared. 'Anyone will do to support you.'

'Anyone will *not* do. We want every character to bear some resemblance to its historical prototype.'

'But no one really knows what the originals looked like. There weren't any photographs in those days and the portraits that exist aren't very reliable.'

'The facial appearance must bear some relation to the known characteristics. In the Henry VIII series the casting was very successful. The main characters were most convincing.'

Esme looked at him from under her eyelashes.

'And your female principals? You've a clear picture of them, of course?'

'Very clear. They're important.'

'Perhaps they're cast already? In fact I believe they are.'

'Then you know more than I do.'

'Perhaps I do. You aren't the only person to decide who they'll be, Aubrey has a very big say-so, and some regard for possible backers.'

'Nevertheless I possess a veto if he chooses someone entirely unsuitable,' Dorian told her suavely.

'Sounds like the United Nations,' Dame Eleanor interposed, sensing tension. 'Some country always vetoes any sensible suggestion, so they never get anywhere, or so it seems to me. I know what Esme's fishing for, and you might do a lot worse.'

'Much worse,' Esme agreed with a meaning smile.

Dorian said nothing. Esme was angling for the principal leading lady, but it would seem she was not his idea of her. Nor was she Jocelyn's. Catherine Swynford, she thought, must have possessed a depth and strength of character beyond Esme's triviality, to have kept her lover so long. She gave a little sigh, wishing she were in the running. So far she had had no opportunity to bring out the full flowering of her talent, and this Plantagenet play appealed to her.

Esme's cold blue eyes turned in her direction.

'From the way Jo's dressed tonight one might suppose she was offering herself for a walk-on,' she said maliciously.

Jocelyn flushed as both Dorian and Dame Eleanor assessed her appearance.

'I suppose the lines of my dress are a little mediaeval,' she said diffidently. 'I hadn't thought of it until now.' Which was not quite true, but she resented Esme's imputation.

Dame Eleanor said musingly, 'It suits you, and at least you would look in the picture. So many modern girls can never look in period.'

'Such an opportunity for Jo,' Esme murmured spitefully. 'All of us here to be impressed.'

Dorian smiled sardonically. 'I've already ascertained that Jocelyn does not make the most of her opportunities,' he observed.

'Really, you do surprise me,' Esme drawled, 'but I

expect her approach is too subtle to be obvious to a mere male.'

Baited beyond endurance, Jocelyn flashed:

'I've no mercenary designs upon Mr Armitage or his play—in fact if he offered me a part, I wouldn't take it.'

'You might change your tune if he did,' Esme said nastily.

'Please,' Dorian protested, 'I'm on holiday and I refuse to discuss shop any further. Now, what are we going to do tomorrow if it stops raining?'

At that moment Mrs McTavish came into dinner accompanied by a friend, and took the table next to theirs. Dorian gave her a friendly smile which she returned with an icy glare. Piqued, he enquired in a low voice:

'What's bitten her? She's always been so forthcoming.'

'She's very nice,' Dorry declared indignantly. 'She thought Mademoiselle Jo was my *maman*, but I told her she wasn't.'

'Oh!' Enlightened, Dorian gave Jocelyn a sly glance.

Esme's plucked eyebrows rose as she glanced from one to the other, noticing Jocelyn's conscious look and Dorian's amusement.

'Seems to be quite time Dame Eleanor joined you,' she said pointedly. 'These unofficial sort of relationships are always misunderstood, and those two women are the sort of cats you find in this sort of one-horse place. I vote we leave for Edinburgh tomorrow, there's some life there; there's nothing here except mountains and water.'

'It's a nice change from London,' Dame Eleanor pointed out. 'Dorian, I've been hoping you'll take me to Skye. I've never been there and it's so romantic, the Road to the Isles and all that.'

'The road to nowhere!' Esme was disgusted by this

suggestion. Then recollecting her manners, she went on sweetly: 'I'm sure so much rough travelling would be too much for you. A really nice hotel in Edinburgh would give you a good rest.'

The old lady snorted: 'I'm not yet decrepit, Esme, and I'd hardly call Dorian's car rough travelling. Go to Edinburgh by all means if you wish, but I shall go to Skye.'

'I'll be delighted to take you,' Dorian told her, 'and Dorry will love the ferry boat.'

He went on to outline their route, Fort William and then along the Road to the Isles to Mallaig, while Esme looked like a thundercloud, and Jocelyn listened with a sinking heart. This then was the parting of the ways. She looked nostalgically round the dining room, her eyes lingering on the table by the window. It had been good while it lasted, but she had always expected it to end when Dorian's friends arrived. That they would consist of his grandmother and Esme had been a surprise, and though she liked Dame Eleanor, she would be very glad to part company with Esme Carr.

Dorry was nodding over his dessert and Dame Eleanor announced that it was time he was in bed.

'I'll take him up,' Jocelyn offered, glad of an excuse to flee from Esme's malevolent glances. 'Come along, Dorry.'

He came with alacrity, and as they moved away, Jocelyn heard Esme say:

'Have you engaged her as a nursemaid, or what?'

She did not hear Dorian's reply, but with her head held high swept past the next table, ignoring the censorious glances of its occupants. At the door, she glanced back. Esme was looking furious, Dorian triumphant and Dame Eleanor amused. She concluded that Miss Carr had made a last plea for a sojourn in Edinburgh and been defeated.

The lift decanted them on the top floor and on impulse, Jocelyn pushed open the door of the sun lounge. The Cobbler's sinister crown was black against the sunset, as they had so often seen it, and the loch was molten copper.

'This is the last time you'll see it,' she said to Dorry. 'You'll be moving on tomorrow.'

'*Bien*, I do not like it, it is *triste*,' Dorry declared. 'I hope Skye will be more comfortable. Will you like Skye, '*mademoiselle*?'

Jocelyn hesitated. If she told him she would not be going with him, he might make a scene and refuse to go to sleep. It would be better to leave him in ignorance of the parting to come until the morrow, so she gave him a non-committal reply.

Her heart was heavy as she settled him in his bed. Tenderly she stroked the smooth black head and hoped fervently that his great-grandmother would be kind to him, while Dorian devoted himself to Esme, as he would surely do if only for commercial reasons. Mr Carr's sponsorship would be valuable towards financing the expensive production he had set his heart upon. That was important to him, she and Esme were not, and he would not scruple to pay court to Esme to gain her father's patronage.

Dorry was soon asleep, but she lingered by his bed. It was too early to retire, but she had no wish to encounter Dorian's travelling companions again. She looked round the room, which tonight showed no sign of Dorian's occupancy. His robe and toilet things were in the bathroom. Dorry's clothes, which she had neatly folded and put upon a chair, were all that met her eye. A woman's room, even in a hotel, would be more revealing. She herself had brought with her a travelling clock, a novel and various cosmetics which littered her dressing table. Yet something of his essence seemed to linger there, a faint whiff of bay rum and after-shave, and she was loth to leave it.

A light tap on the door aroused her from her reverie and Dame Eleanor pushed it open, putting her head round it.

'Is he asleep?' she asked in a penetrating stage whisper.

Jocelyn nodded and rose to her feet. She had no excuse to remain dreaming about Dorian, and she walked out into the passage.

'I always leave the door slightly ajar,' she said, 'so if he wakes and calls I'll hear him.'

'Then do you sit in the passage all evening?' the old lady demanded.

'Oh no, I stay in the sun lounge. I'd hear him from there.'

Together they went through the swing door. Dame Eleanor had changed from her travelling clothes into a hostess gown of brilliant paisley pattern. A white shawl was wrapped about her shoulders, and long earrings tinkled in her ears. She was an impressive figure. The lounge was empty, the last light lingering on the view beyond the huge windows.

'I like it here,' Dame Eleanor said, subsiding into an easy chair facing the loch. 'Ring for coffee, will you, I'll have it here with you.' Jocelyn hastened to obey, and she went on: 'I'm glad we've got it to ourselves. I suppose most of the guests prefer the bar at this hour. I wanted to talk to you.'

'I'm honoured, madam,' Jocelyn told her, sitting down beside her.

'Zut, don't stand on ceremony with me, I'm only an old woman, a—what do you call us nowadays?—a senior citizen,' she chuckled. 'Modern youth has no patience with age, it likes to segregate everyone into so-called age groups, and mine isn't yours.'

'I ... I find older people interesting,' Jocelyn faltered, rather taken aback by these remarks.

'Well-mannered if insincere,' was the old lady's comment. 'No, don't protest,' as Jocelyn was about to speak, 'that wasn't what I wanted to talk about. I must confess I was shattered by Dorian's news. I thought he was committed to Esme. I'm afraid he's cooked his goose with her, but he assures me he can find other backers less exigent than Reggie Carr. I must say you're a great improvement on that painted little doll.'

Jocelyn stared at her blankly.

'I ... I'm afraid I don't understand.'

'No need to pretend, my child, even if it is being kept a secret. Dorian has told me all about it—he and I have always been close. I quite understand how you shrink from publicity, but I shan't blurt it abroad.' She ran her eyes over the girl's slim graceful figure outlined by the clinging blue dress, the richness of her hair, her slender neck and smoky blue eyes, so different from Esme's hard round orbs. 'You're quite beautiful and it's obvious Dorian adores you, so I can't blame him.'

The entrance of a waiter with a tray of coffee checked further conversation. At the old lady's request, Jocelyn poured out for her, while the man collected some used glasses.

'White or black?' Jocelyn asked mechanically, her thoughts in a whirl.

'Black, and two lumps of sugar. Oh, I see it's in those nasty paper packets. I hate this mania for wrapping everything up. Even the butter is in tinfoil. It never tastes the same to me.'

The waiter withdrew, as Jocelyn handed the old lady her cup.

'Now,' she said firmly, 'will you please tell me what you were talking about?'

'Of course Dorian had to tell us to stop Esme pursuing him. After you'd gone with Dorry, he informed us that you and he were engaged.'

Jocelyn's spoon rattled against her saucer. Engaged?

Why had Dorian told such a lie? Was it to shield her from malicious gossip? But he had said he did not mind about that. Or was it as his grandmother had suggested, to score off Esme, because he was not pleased by her appearance at Arrochar and resented her efforts to annex him? To tell her Jocelyn was his fiancée was the sort of rebuff that would appeal to his sardonic humour, even though it was likely to cost him dear if her father withdrew his support for his play. Whatever had motivated him, he had shown scant regard for her feelings, and surely he could not imagine she would lend herself to a bogus engagement simply to rid him of an incubus.

Dame Eleanor was regarding her with a satirical smile that was oddly like her grandson's. Did she suspect that the engagement was a fake?

On the verge of an emphatic denial, Jocelyn checked herself. The explanation, if explanation there were, should come from Dorian; his grandmother might not believe she was in earnest, attributing her repudiation to bashfulness, for what girl in her senses would refuse to accept the invincible Dorian Armitage? While she hesitated, Mrs McTavish and her friend came into the lounge, precluding further private conversation. The woman gave Jocelyn a beaming smile, so that she realised with a sinking heart that the news had already filtered through the hotel. But that did not really matter as they would all be leaving next day.

'She's evidently thinking it's never too late to mend,' Dame Eleanor whispered with a chuckle. 'I'm afraid your devotion to Dorry put you in a compromising situation, but now Dorian has declared himself, you're in the clear.'

'As if that mattered!' Jocelyn said angrily. 'I do wish people would mind their own business.'

She glared at Mrs McTavish, not caring if she overheard, and the Scotswoman smiled back at her ingratiatingly, so evidently she had not.

Dame Eleanor's expressive dark eyes gleamed mischievously.

'Such people justify themselves by considering they are guardians of public morality,' she murmured.

'But surely you don't think...' Jocelyn began.

'I think nothing,' her companion interrupted quickly, 'but I do know my grandson rather well. You won't find him easy to manage.'

'No, I don't imagine I should. By the way, where is he?'

'He went out for a stroll. He felt the need to cool off after Esme's tantrums. She's leaving first thing in the morning, by the way. Poor dear, so much energy expended for nothing, but really that young woman has no proper pride.'

Jocelyn looked out at the view before them. The sky was mauve and blue behind the Cobbler and lights in the streets were piercing the long northern twilight. It was never really dark at midsummer in that latitude.

'Is she in love with him?' she asked bluntly.

'She's in love with the glamour that surrounds a famous actor,' Dame Eleanor told her tartly. She glanced at Mrs McTavish and lowered her voice. 'If Dorian were a nobody she'd have no use for him. Also she wants to star in his play.'

'I suppose she could still do that.'

'Unfortunately for her Dorian doesn't see her in the part she wants. I thought you'd have gathered that.'

'Has he any idea who he does want to play it?' Jocelyn asked curiously, temporarily diverted from her own dilemma.

I think he has someone in mind, but Aubrey will insist that their leading lady is a box office draw.'

'And she isn't well known?'

'I mustn't say any more. Oh, I'm sure you're discreet, but we don't want any leaks at this stage. When Dorian gets back to London he'll be holding auditions.'

'Oh, of course.' Jocelyn felt rebuked. She had not meant to press for advance information, but she could not resist broaching the subject that was so important to herself. 'Do you think I've any chance of getting a small part, or even a walk-on?' she enquired diffidently.

'My dear child,' Dame Eleanor looked almost shocked, 'surely that's between you and your fiancé? I don't suppose Dorian would allow his wife to appear in a crowd. It's hardly suitable.'

That jolted Jocelyn back to her present impossible situation. Dame Eleanor's reference to Dorian's wife had caused her a pang. That she would never be, and it was too bad that she might be done out of a much-needed professional engagement on account of this absurd trick he was playing upon her. Oberon playing destiny again, she thought disdainfully, or more like Puck. He had adroitly got rid of Esme at her expense, but she was not going to allow him to futher involve her in whatever further mischief he was contemplating.

Rising to her feet, she said distractedly:

'If you'll excuse me, I'll go and look for Dorian. I've something to say to him.'

'Naturally,' her companion murmured with a wink. 'But what about Dorian Junior? Haven't you appointed youself unofficial baby-minder?'

Jocelyn hesitated. 'He doesn't usually wake once he's gone off.'

Dame Eleanor laughed. 'I'll stay here until you come back, so run along, my dear. We can't let poor Dorry stand between two ardent lovers!'

Jocelyn hurried away, her face flaming. Dorian was not her lover, nor ever would be, and if he thought this pseudo-engagement would present an opportunity to break down her resistance, he was going to find himself very much mistaken. Her feeling for him was too deep and sincere to be desecrated by such a ruse. All she was to him was a passing fancy, a midsummer idyll to be forgotten when he returned to work, and she was not going to allow him to break her heart when he abandoned her, as he surely would if she were weak enough to give in to him.

CHAPTER FIVE

JOCELYN descended in the lift and stepped out into the floodlit car park without waiting to put on a coat, being too agitated to recollect that the evening would be chilly. Even in late June a thin dress with minute sleeves and low neck was inadequate protection against the Highland night air.

She crossed the tarmac and descended into the street, which went past the hotel at a slightly lower level. A line of villas and cottages separated it from the loch, but its further shore was visible over the low roof of a bungalow. A distant caravan camp on the opposite hill side sprinkled the foothills with a spangle of lights, above which the mountains rose in night-shaded majesty, shutting out the stars. The water still glimmered palely, reflecting the fading afterglow; to her left, a glowworm thread along the dark hillside marked the passage of a late train to Glasgow.

Shivering a little, Jocelyn stood irresolute, looking to north and south, for she did not know in which direction Dorian had gone. She had embarked upon a wild goose chase, for he might have taken it into his head to walk as far as Tarbet and it would be a long time before he returned.

She was loth to go back inside, for the peace and quiet of the windless evening was soothing to her overstrung nerves. Behind her light blossomed in the many windows of the hotel as the guests began to retire; from the bar came the muted sound of music. This was to be her last night at Arrochar. She had thought so before, but this time she would allow nothing to detain her—besides, Dorian and his family were leaving in the morning. She would join George and Ronald for the last part of her holiday and put the actor out of her mind.

George had rung up once since his departure to ask how she was faring, and she had given him a bright account of her doings, omitting to mention that Dorian had accompanied her and her charge upon their expeditions. There was, she had justified her concealment, no need to worry him by arousing unwarrantable suspicions. True, Dorian had made a pass at her, but she had, as she had so often told her father, proved equal to the situation. Now all danger was past, for on the morrow their ways would part.

She glanced up at the hotel. Esme Carr was still there, and though Dame Eleanor had said she was leaving also next morning for Edinburgh, it was possible she would endeavour to make Dorian change his mind about going to Skye before she left, ignoring the news of his engagement. From what she knew of the actress's character, Esme was too confident of the power of her own attractions to believe Dorian could withstand a further assault in favour of her insignificant self. That, Jocelyn thought, was an error in tactics. Dorian was by nature a hunter and did not appreciate the role of the quarry. Esme had acted too blatantly by pursuing him to Scotland. She supposed it was her own lack of response to his overtures that had intrigued him in her own case. Perhaps she had been foolish to allow her fastidiousness to stand between them. He could have given her fulfilment ... of a sort. He had told her she expected too much of life and she should take, as he expressed it, what came along, as he did himself. She had come along but had refused to be taken. On the whole she was glad that she had maintained her integrity.

As for their fictitious engagement which had brought her out full of protest in search of him, it had been a chivalrous effort to shield her good name from the malice of Mrs McTavish and her cronies, because he felt that to endanger her reputation was a poor return for her care of Dorry. He was not without finer impulses, and he knew very well it would cease upon the morrow. One of the shortest engagements upon record, she thought wryly. He would tell Dame Eleanor that she had had to rejoin her family, and by the time they all returned to London, the incident would have faded away.

All this being so, there was no point in standing shivering in the cold waiting to waylay Dorian. Her first indignant reaction to his supposed presumption had died down. She had much better go to bed, and if, in the morning, she met with any opposition, which she did not expect, she could as a last resort, and to satisfy Dame Eleanor, say that George had met with a slight accident.

As she turned to go back, a car came down the street, its headlights illuminating her figure and temporarily blinding her. As she paused in bewilderment, a familiar voice hailed her from behind it.

'Jocelyn, what are you doing out here?'

'I was looking for you,' she admitted, unable to think of an excuse. The sight of his dimly seen figure and the sound of his voice had caused her heart to leap and throw her into momentary confusion.

'Is something wrong?' Dorian asked anxiously. 'My grandmother? Dorry?'

'No, oh no, they're quite all right. I ... I wanted to speak to you alone.'

His fingers closed over her bare arm, which she was sure must be covered with goose-pimples.

'Was it so important you had to freeze yourself?' he

demanded. 'Didn't you have the sense to put on a coat or something?'

He was so close to her in the intimate darkness that she could not think coherently.

'I . . . I didn't think,' she murmured vaguely.

He laughed. 'Something has upset you?'

'It had . . . but upon sober reflection . . .'

'No, I don't want to hear your sober reflections,' he cut in, his voice half tender, half mocking, that musical vibrant voice that seemed to express so much more than he meant, and always touched her heart's chords. With his face unseen, it became doubly potent. 'What you felt in the heat of the moment will be much more interesting, and I can guess what has disturbed you. But there's no need to freeze while you unburden yourself. Let's get into my car, it'll be warmer.'

Dislodging his hand, she said frigidly: 'No, thank you. I've decided I've nothing to say, and I'm going inside.'

'No, you're not.' To stay her he caught her round the waist, encircling her with a firm grip. 'It's too populous inside, and we must have a little private talk before we go on to Skye. Will you please do as I say.'

The close clasp of his arm holding her against his side played havoc with Jocelyn's nerves. She could not, she dared not sit beside him in the confined space of his car. He seemed to be in one of his most arrogant moods, and she had been a fool to come to look for him—she had no defence against his physical charm. As if sensing her reluctance and its cause, he said derisively:

'You can sit in the back seat if you fear my proximity will disturb your concentration upon what you have to say.'

'I'm not in the least afraid of you,' she said mendaciously, as he guided her towards the car, his arm tightening so that she had perforce to accompany him.

She hoped he would not notice her irregular breathing.

'That isn't quite what I meant,' he retorted. 'Good lord, girl, how thin you are!' He gave her waist a tight squeeze before releasing her to unlock the car.

'Caveman stuff,' she gasped.

'Not at all.' He opened the door to the rear seat. 'I know my Tarzan classics better than that. I should drag you to my lair by the hair of your head—you appear to have enough by the way to make that feat possible—and when I'd got you there . . . well, you can guess the rest. Please to get in. I'll turn the heater on, but while it warms up, you can wrap yourself in the rug that's on the seat. There's no need for you to be frozen outside as well as inside, my little icicle.'

If he knew how fast her pulses were hammering, he would not call her that, Jocelyn thought as she got into the car. Mercifully he did not. Her body was still conscious of his close grip, though he no longer held her. She leaned back against the upholstery, as he closed the door upon her, pulling the rug around her. She was going to need to preserve an icy calm if she hoped to keep control of the situation. She had been crazy to allow him to manoeuvre her into this position. Why had she not stayed in the security of the hotel? It was going to be very difficult to broach the question of their alleged engagement alone with him in the night. It would be much better not to bring it up at all, but she doubted if she would be able to avoid it now.

Dorian stepped into the driver's seat and started the engine. He let it run for a few moments and warm air from the heater began to percolate through the car. Then he pushed in the gear lever and the car slid away from the hotel.

'Can't we stay here?' Jocelyn asked, alarmed.

'I prefer to find a spot where we'll be safe from interruption,' he returned ominously.

He drove fast over the neck of land that separated the two lochs. Loch Lomond, being wider and more open, still reflected the sky, where the aftermath of the summer's day still lingered in the west. In the east the radiance above the hills proclaimed the rising moon. Ben Lomond was a humped dark mass against it, but the water glimmered pewter and black at its foot.

'A twilit faërie world,' Dorian observed, as he drove along the lake side.

Jocelyn made no rejoinder; she did not want enchantment to aid her in her coming ordeal, but sound common sense.

They came to a layby, and Dorian drew off the road, shutting off his engine. There was little traffic at that hour and silent stillness enwrapped them. Even the trees were for once motionless.

Dorian put his arm over the back of the seat that divided them and turned towards her.

'Well, what is it that you wanted to say to me before you had your sober reflections?'

The interior of the car was dark, only a faint grey luminosity coming through the windows. Wrapped in the thick tartan rug, Jocelyn was undiscernible to her questioner and he to her; but though she could not see him she was painfully aware of his presence. She was glad that he could not see her face. Something of her former indignation returned to her, as she demanded:

'I'd like to know by what right you've told everybody we're engaged!'

'Is that all?' he sounded amused. 'I thought some major catastrophe had occurred. I didn't tell everybody, as you say, only Esme and Gran.'

'One of them must have broadcast it. Mrs McTavish, I believe that's her name, certainly knew.'

'Ah,' he sighed with satisfaction. 'I'm glad it's got round to her.'

'Yes ... well, you might have consulted me first. How

do you think I felt when Dame Eleanor sprang it on me?'

'Grateful I hope.' Now his voice became stern. 'Did you think I'd let that McTavish besom throw mud at you, especially after you'd been so kind looking after Dorry?'

'I'm afraid she believed we'd gone rather far for an engaged couple. She saw me coming out of your room.'

'So I surmised, but in Scotland, certainly in the rural areas, a handfasting is considered as good as a marriage, so her nasty suspicions should be allayed.'

Jocelyn began to laugh. 'You're very virtuous all of a sudden,' she observed. 'If you'd had your way ...' and she broke off, overcome by sudden embarrassment.

'Well, it's too bad to be gunned when we're perfectly innocent,' he exclaimed, adding regretfully, 'Unfortunately.'

'From your point of view?'

'That's beside the point. But I've been indiscreet, Jocelyn. I'm usually more careful, so I took the simplest way of remedying the situation. I hope the woman has changed her tune?'

'Oh, she has. It's awfully sweet of you, Dorian to be concerned for my reputation. I wasn't really worried, my conscience being clear—but suppose the press get hold of it? Won't that be awkward for you?'

'I'll survive; it won't be the first time the papers have linked my name with a charming lady and had to admit they were mistaken,' Dorian told her sardonically. 'But as I'm not a pop singer or even a television star my love life isn't spectacular enough to hit the headlines. We won't give any interviews,' he added warningly.

'Of course not. But if you've quarrelled with Esme Carr upon my account, won't that be harmful to you? I mean, you needed her or rather her father's goodwill to help with your play.'

'I can do without it. I wasn't prepared to pay Esme's price. Good God, Jocelyn, do you imagine I'd sell myself to her, even for the sake of my play?'

Jocelyn felt an unworthy but very natural glow of pleasure to hear Esme so dismissed. She had suffered from 'Titania's' cattiness during the run of *The Dream.*

'Then your play won't be jeopardised?' she asked anxiously.

'It would be if I allowed Esme to murder Catherine'.

A reply that startled Jocelyn, who had been imagining Miss Carr was seeking a more intimate connection with Dorian, but apparently all the actress was after was the lead in the Plantagenet play. Possibly the two went together. Love scenes played on the stage could be carried over into real life. He had in the beginning been very attentive to his Titania, until he had grown tired of her. An actor's world was comprised of artificiality and illusion. But if he had had an affair with Esme he had soon discarded her, and he seemed determined not to become involved with her again.

The gratitude she had felt when he had expressed his remorse for compromising her faded before this less attractive aspect of him. She must always remember that Dorian Armitage was incurably fickle.

'Have you decided who you do want for the part?' she asked, wondering if that lady was destined to be the next object of his wandering affections.

'We considered——' he mentioned the well known name of a much married actress, 'but she's under contract elsewhere. We've one or two possibilities to audition when I return to London, but I doubt if any of them have the right quality. In fact the only actress I know who seems to have it is, I'm afraid, out of the question.'

'Why so?'

'She's unknown and therefore would be too big a gamble.'

'Too bad.' She meant it. It was too bad this unknown could not be given her chance.

'Not that I'm averse to taking a gamble,' Dorian told her. 'But Aubrey will insist upon playing safe, and though I'm risking more than I can really spare on this production, I have to consider other people's purses. The others want a big name, but they might remember,' he laughed, 'that it's I who will have to make love to the lady.'

'After all, it's only acting, and isn't it better not to be emotionally involved?'

'That's a moot point. I certainly wouldn't find it helpful to have to simulate fiery passion for some actress who wasn't at all my idea of Catherine Swynford.'

'But Esme Carr wasn't your idea of Titania—you called her insipid, I seem to remember.'

'She was like a fairy doll on top of a Christmas tree, but the audience found her adequate, and you recall that Oberon's attitude towards her was more often vindictive than affectionate. Anyway, I didn't take that romp very seriously.'

It had had serious repercussions for Jocelyn. It was then that he had taken hold of her imagination.

The light had brightened as the moon became visible, a huge golden ball resting on a shoulder of hill. Dorian's form began to take shape; she could see the outline of his head and shoulders and catch the gleam of his eyes. Their conversation had reminded her that he was at the top of his profession while she was only a humble general utility, though she had played one or two of the long parts she had understudied at the repertory when 'flu had struck the cast. Once they were back in their own world he would barely spare her an acknowledgement if they chanced to meet. Yet ironically, at that moment she was posing as his fiancée. She smiled to herself in the darkness, reflecting that their association had been full of strange twists. Tonight she had gone to meet him full of surging resentment, to be followed by apprehension, and they had ended by having an amicable discussion about the theatre.

'I shall look forward to seeing you on your first night,' she told him, for she would have that to which to look forward. He would look wonderful in mediaeval dress.

'That's looking a long way ahead. More immediately I have to convey my cortège to Skye, since my old lady is so set upon it. It looks like being fine tomorrow, I was hoping it would be as I want Gran to see the hills and lochs at their best during the long run up to Fort William.'

'You'll break your journey there?'

'For one night only. We haven't much time left. We'll spend a night or two at Mallaig and then I'm afraid it's back to the grindstone.'

'But aren't you itching to get started on your play?'

Inwardly she was fighting a sense of desolation. His trip would not include her and by the time she was back in London, Dorry might have forgotten her.

'Of course I am, but a period of relaxation is not only pleasant but necessary. Well, if I've answered all your queries, we'd better be getting back. We'll need to get away early tomorrow.'

'And our brief engagement will be over,' she said a little wistfully.

'Oh, no, it won't. As long as we're travelling together we'd better preserve the fiction, it gives you more ... er ... status. No one would believe you're Dorry's nannie.'

'We shan't be travelling together. If you'd give me a lift as far as Fort William, I'd be grateful, but it's time, high time,' she emphasised the last two words, 'I joined my people. You've given me a wonderful week, Mr

Armitage, and I'm grateful, but I can't presume upon your generosity any longer.'

'If you persist in Mr Armitaging me I'll get into the back of the car and do something you won't like,' he threatened.

'Very well, Dorian,' she said meekly. It did not matter with parting so near.

'That's better. You really can be provoking, Jocelyn. Now, as regards this journey of ours, of course you must come with us. I'd never have undertaken it if I thought you were going to back out. I'm counting upon you to help look after Dorry and Gran. They're too heavy a responsibility for one lone man. Gran might be taken ill or Dorry might hurt himself. They need you, Jocelyn, you're quite indispensable.'

She wavered in her resolution. This was no amorous appeal, but genuine anxiety; he feared an old woman and a young child might be something of a burden to manage singlehanded.

'I don't even know what clothes the kid should wear,' he said plaintively. 'And they always seem to be dirty.'

Jocelyn laughed. She had several times washed out Dorry's smalls, but surely he could enlist the services of a chambermaid? She told him so.

'I'd only be told the hotel wasn't a laundry. Don't be so hard hearted, Jocelyn.'

'Then take them to a cleaners, most of them do a twenty-four-hour service.'

'They won't where we're going.' He dropped his light manner, and said seriously: 'Do come, I'm certain you'll enjoy it.'

'I'm sure I should, but that's not the point, and I'm sure Dame Eleanor could cope with Dorry's wardrobe —she seems a very capable person in spite of her age. You've already told me not to try to monopolise Dorry. Oh, yes, you did,' as he gave an impatient exclamation, 'and I feel that as a guest I'd be an imposition.'

'Will you stop talking rubbish? You know they both want you to come, and of course you're welcome as our guest. Gran thinks you're my fiancée, and regards you, a little prematurely perhaps, as one of the family.' He shifted his position in the car, trying to pierce the gloom that enshrouded her. 'What on earth would you do with yourself at Fort William while your father and brother are breaking their necks on Ben Nevis? It'll only be for a few days, anyhow.'

Jocelyn began to weaken. She very much wanted to go, but prudence had restrained her, but as he had said, it was only for a few days and the question of Dorry's clothes had introduced a prosaic element which was far from the sentimental one she feared. She twisted a corner of the rug with nervous fingers while she sought to make up her mind. The moon, no longer gold but silver, was shedding more light as it rode up the sky, the loch had become an argent sheet. Dorian's face had become visible, a black and white mask, but through the shadow under his brows she caught the glitter of his eyes. He was watching her intently and it seemed her decision really was important to him.

'If it's a question of expense——' he began, and she quickly said it was not. She had saved for this holiday and her father was helping her.

'That's my privilage,' he objected, and pointed out that since she was looking after Dorry, the least he could do was to pay her hotel bills.

'Very well,' she agreed, knowing that they would be high. Dame Eleanor would expect the best accommodation procurable.

Then realising he must believe that she had capitulated, she began to protest anew.

'Seriously though, Dorian, it would be better if I didn't come with you. It . . . it isn't awfully wise.'

'Now what the hell do you mean by that?' he demanded with exasperation.

A few more days in his company, tempting though the prospect was, would only involve her more deeply with him, nor did she altogether trust him. Their pseudo-engagement put her in an invidious position of which he might seek to take advantage, and if he importuned her again she did not know if she would have the strength to resist him.

'I should think my meaning was obvious,' she retorted tartly. 'You've already got yourself an unwanted fiancée and you've yet to think up some reason for discarding me to present to your grandmother before we go back to London.' She glanced half hopefully at his shadowed face but it was as enigmatical as carved marble. 'It would be so much easier if we told her I had to join my family.'

'Most unconvincing.'

'I don't see it, and what would you do if I sued you for breach of promise? I might be inspired to do so if we continue with this ... er charade.'

'Breach of promise is obsolete,' he returned impassively. 'I'm not afraid you'll ever be able to embarrass me.'

There was a pause while she reflected a little bitterly that she was the one who might suffer embarrassment.

'Well, have you any more futile arguments to trot out?' he asked with a touch of arrogance. 'You'll have to dream up something better than you've done so far before I'll let you go.'

A quiver ran through her at his tone. Believing he had won, he was becoming masterful. If only he meant he really wanted to hold her and was not merely making a convenience out of her!

Suddenly she tired of the conflict. Why continue to withstand him, when she so much wanted to go?

'No, I've nothing more to say,' she said wearily. 'I accept your kind offer, and I'll do my best for Dorry and Dame Eleanor.'

'Excellent, but don't sound so glum,' he chided her. 'They won't make a slave of you, and I'm very grateful for your co-operation.'

So he should be, she thought, for she would be freeing him to seek more lively company than that of an old woman and a young child, who were not ideal companions for a virile active man, but she also was young and enjoyed bathing and dancing. So far his company had compensated for the lack of them, but if he withdrew, she would have no opportunity to make any dates. Not that she really wanted to, but with a vague idea of pointing out to him that she was making a small sacrifice in return for his bounty, she said:

'But I *am* on holiday, and I wouldn't have minded a little fun.'

'One comes to the West Highlands to admire the scenery,' he remarked drily, 'and you'll have plenty of opportunities to do that.'

He leaned a little further over the seat back, and his voice sank to a caressing murmur.

'As for fun, as you call it, do I detect regret in your voice? I offered you that too, you know, but you weren't interested. Have you changed your mind?'

'No, I didn't mean that,' she cried, realising she had expressed herself badly.

'Then what did you mean?' He laughed softly.

With an effort, Jocelyn drew herself up straight against the back of the car, and said deliberately:

'I don't buy second-hand goods.'

A tense silence followed this thrust, which she regretted almost as soon as she had uttered it. Dorian had turned away from her and was sitting very still with his back to her. It was a nasty thing to have said and Dorian hardly deserved it. She clasped her hands together and found she was trembling. Somewhere in the trees beside them an owl hooted, the mournful sound echoing across the quiet waters.

At length Dorian spoke, coldly and acidly, without turning his head.

'I suppose you consider I deserved that rap, but may I point out that you know nothing of my private life beyond my unfortunate marriage and the garbled reports in the popular press. You're not the person to judge me, for you're a mass of absurd inhibitions and old-fashioned prejudices. I say absurd, because you aspire to be an actress. It will do you and your art a great deal of good when someone succeeds in breaking them down, and one day someone will. But it won't be me. From henceforth I will treat you with the chill courtesy that you seem to prefer, because I need your help with my child and my grandmother, and I want you to come to Skye. But under different circumstances,' a note of quiet savagery crept into his voice, 'I would do to you what needs to be done before you come alive—melt the ice that covers your emotions and make you as mad for my kisses as you now pretend to disdain them. There's fire in you, my girl, that only waits to be ignited, and a night in a man's arms would be a revelation to you.'

The interior of the car seemed to throb with the intensity of his utterance and Jocelyn's heart beat wildly in response. The tension increased until she felt she must scream, though Dorian remained motionless, gazing out of the windscreen. She had an odd illusion that he was actually embracing her, she could hardly breathe and a vice seemed clamped about her ribs. Auto-suggestion, she thought distractedly; that low, vibrant voice had mesmerised her.

The owl hooted again and its dark shape on noiseless wings swooped across the loch. The sound broke the spell that bound her and she drew a long breath of relief. Dorian was a superb actor and he had brought the full force of his art and his magnetic personality to bear upon her. It had been a very moving performance, but that was all it was. He knew his power and had wanted to make her feel it.

'Very dramatic,' she said with a slight tremor in her voice. 'Do you expect me to applaud it?'

His outburst seemed to have expended his spleen, for he turned round and said lightly:

'I apologise for an histrionic piece of ham. We actors are apt to over-dramatise our emotions. The artistic temperament, you know.'

'I don't know, most of my efforts have been confined to what's called general utility, though I did once play Juliet. In that capacity we have to learn to keep our tempers.'

'Meaning I lost mine? But you gave me provocation. Forget it. So it's settled you're coming with us to Skye?'

'I don't know if I dare after that furious display.'

'It won't happen again. I promise you I'll keep my distance. I won't even exert a fiancé's privileges.'

'Must we continue with that pretence?' she asked quickly.

'Definitely. I've yet to find an excuse for jilting you. Besides, Gran is enjoying our supposed idyll—'say's you're such a nice girl.' An edge crept into his voice. 'It won't hurt you to play up to her when she's around, but when she isn't, you won't mind if I seek other distractions? I don't doubt I can find someone to appreciate me, even if I am shop-soiled.'

Though he spoke lightly Jocelyn knew then she had wounded his vanity beyond forgiveness by her unfortunate remark. She also had an uneasy suspicion that he knew she was not as indifferent as she pretended to be. He would deliberately pay court to some other girl to punish her, while persisting in the farce of their engagement to humiliate her, and at the same time exacting service from her for his dependants. She was sure he would not miss any opportunity to wound her if he could. He was showing the inhuman quality he had used so successfully in his interpretation of Oberon, and she remembered his vindictive expression in the play when he had said:

'Wake when some vile thing is near.'

She was sure it would give him profound satisfaction to see her besotted by some ass-headed monstrosity, and all the more so if it was through his agency. She should have been repelled, but she was not. Cruel he might be, but he fascinated her, and she was still drawn to him by the blind unreason of her love.

The sensible thing to do would be to cry off, even if she had more or less given her promise, but she was assailed by a sudden recklessness. A certain stubbornness in her nature rejected defeat; she would show him how little she cared.

'I could still refuse to come with you,' she said coolly. 'But I feel I've been challenged, so I'll play my part. After all you've just said, I'm assured that you won't pester me with unwanted gallantries.'

Dorian seemed about to say something, changed his mind, and guided the car back on to the road. With its bonnet towards home, he slammed his foot down upon the accelerator which indicated she had again aroused his temper. It was fortunate they encountered no other vehicle on the narrow road during their mad career, or their story would have ended then and there.

CHAPTER SIX

JOCELYN was awakened early next morning by a loud rapping on her door and Dorry's shrill voice calling:

'Open! Open, Mademoiselle Jo, *vite, vite*!'

Aroused from a confused dream in which she had been pursued through a dark forest by a faunlike creature with Dorian's features, she wondered if some emergency had arisen, and reaching for her dressing gown, she hastened to open the door. Dorry, dressed in shorts and jersey, his hair wet from his ablutions, was standing on the threshold wriggling with impatience. He surveyed her negligée, her long hair in two plaits, with evident disapproval.

'Aren't you dressed, *mademoiselle*? Papa has been up for ages and ages. He says we have many miles to go, and if we don't hurry we won't have time for breakfast. I'm hungry and I can't get my case to shut.'

Jocelyn tried to rub the sleep out of her eyes while she assimilated this information.

'It's still very early, little one. I'll come along as soon as I've showered. From the noise you made I thought something dreadful had happened.'

'But it will if I haven't time for breakfast. Papa's luggage is all ready to be put in the car, but he might go before mine is packed, and you know how he hates to have to wait.'

'He can't be in such a desperate hurry,' Jocelyn remarked, thinking that Dame Eleanor would not be up yet. 'As soon as I've washed I'll be able to help you, and I'll make sure you have your breakfast.'

'Can I wait in here while you wash?' Dorry asked, being familiar with her room. 'I like this room better than mine.'

Jocelyn agreed and collecting clothes departed for the bathroom. Dorry panicked so easily. Dorian would never leave before he was fed. During the hours it had taken her to go to sleep, she had almost decided to tell Dorian that she had changed her mind. Those few intense moments of emotion by the loch had shaken her. He had too much power over her. But in the prosaic light of early morning the experience had become a fantastic dream, and here was Dorry, showing how much he depended upon her.

She returned to her room, bathed and dressed in trousers with a light short-sleeved sweater and her hair knotted in the nape of her neck. Dorry was amusing himself switching her bedside lamp on and off.

'Better not do that, you'll fuse it,' she told him. 'Come and help me pack.'

She opened her half-filled case and instructed him to hand her the articles to be stowed inside.

'You haven't any *bijoux*,' he remarked. 'Maman had lots of them. She kept them in a locked box.'

Presents from Dorian, Jocelyn supposed, and as she glanced at her bare fingers it occurred to her that if he wished to preserve this fiction of an engagement, he ought to give her a ring. That she did not want him to do, for it would be a meaningless token which she would have to return at the end of the holiday. Anxious to forestall him, she dived into her case and fished out the little cardboard box in which she kept her few trinkets. From it she extracted a ring which she sometimes wore in the evenings, a simple silver band enclosing a polished stone. It was pretty but of no value. She slipped it on to the appropriate finger, wondering if Dorry knew its significance, but apparently he did not, as he made no comment, and in any case his mother, being French, would wear her rings on her right hand.

But while she continued packing he looked at it disparagingly.

'It does not sparkle like Maman's rings did.'

Elise Armitage would have worn precious stones, probably diamonds, and the young Dorian would have had to stretch his money to buy her a ring that he thought worthy of her. Involuntarily Jocelyn asked:

'Was your mother very pretty?'

His face lit up. 'She had hair like sunshine and she always smelled so nice, but she did not like me to kiss her, for fear I rumple her.' His small face puckered. 'She did not come often to see me, and in Paris she was always going out. It was Nounou *qui j'aimais*.'

Jocelyn fastened her case, having gathered a comprehensive picture of Elise. She seemed to have been a frivolous, worthless creature, preferring her gay life in Paris to making a home for her husband, and neglecting her child. Her desertion partly excused Dorian's present tendencies and explained his low opinion of women. He had come to regard them as objects of pleasure and had no desire to form a permanent connection with another one.

'Now will you please come and shut *my* case,' Dorry demanded imperiously. At times he reminded Jocelyn very much of his father.

She hesitated. 'Your father is outside?'

'But yes, Mademoiselle Jo, filling up the car and packing the boot.' He could never understand her reluctance to enter his room if there were any chance of meeting its co-occupant.

Dorian had already removed his things; Dorry's case was in the middle of the floor, half-open with his pyjamas, slippers and sponge bag stuffed in anyhow so that it would not close. Jocelyn soon put that to rights, snapped the hasps, and he proceeded to lug it towards the lift.

'It's too heavy for you, Dorry,' she expostulated. 'Leave it and I'll ring for the porter.'

'No, *mademoiselle,* he take too long to come.'

Nothing would content him but that she fetch her own luggage and put it with his in the lift. Then it transpired that his desperate haste was less upon his father's account than because of his eagerness to leave the Cobbler behind and cross in the ferry to Skye.

Leaving their cases in the vestibule, they went into the dining room, where Dorian had already breakfasted. Jocelyn discovered that Dame Eleanor had had hers sent to her room. There was no sign of Esme Carr and it occurred to Jocelyn that Dorian was in a hurry because he wanted to be gone before she appeared.

He came in as they were finishing their meal with a request that Jocelyn would go upstairs and lend his grandmother a hand. He spoke almost brusquely and did not meet her eyes. Jocelyn thought wryly that it was a good thing Mrs McTavish was not present. His manner was hardly that of a doting fiancé and indicated that he was still incensed with her. Even Dorry noticed, and said triumphantly:

'I told you Papa would be cross because you were so slow.'

Much too slow, but not in the sense that the child meant.

Dame Eleanor was on the first floor and though she was up and dressed her room was strewn with her belongings—an unnecessary amount of unpacking for a one-night stand, she admitted, but she liked to make herself feel at home. By her bed was a silver frame containing a coloured photograph of Dorian as Oberon.

'Not his most rewarding role,' Dame Eleanor stated, 'but I've never seen him look more beautiful.'

She handed the frame to Jocelyn to put in one of

her cases.

Beautiful was the operative word, the girl thought as she stowed it away, though handsome was usually the one applied to a man. It was how she would always remember him when this tour was over, as she had first seen him when he had made such an indelible impression upon her heart and imagination, King of an enchanted realm.

In spite of Dorian's haste, they did not escape without encoutnering Esme. She was in the vestibule when Jocelyn came out of the lift laden with extra coats and bags in Dame Eleanor's wake. That lady seemed to have brought most of her wardrobe with her. Dorian had come in to meet them and been waylaid. Esme was asking him to run her to the station before setting off. Jocelyn heard him say:

'I really haven't time. Surely you can get a taxi?'

'I don't suppose they possess such a thing in this outlandish spot,' Esme pouted. She saw Jocelyn standing behind Dame Eleanor and her eyes narrowed.

'Your fiancée is most obliging. I wouldn't let any man make me into a beast of burden.'

'She likes to be useful,' Dorian returned offhandedly, giving Jocelyn a fleeting glance, but not offering to relieve her of her load. 'Please take them out to the car.' He gave Dame Eleanor his arm. 'You don't travel light, do you, Gran? I hardly think you'll need your fur coat at midsummer.' It hung over Jocelyn's arm.

'The weather is always unpredictable,' the old lady declared. 'I thought there might be snow in the mountains.'

'This isn't Switzerland,' Esme sneered, 'and Jo's a doormat.' She stared at her insolently. 'Dor'll soon get tired of you,' she muttered. 'He likes a bit of spirit.'

Dorian and Dame Eleanor had passed out of earshot, and Esme, her poison spent, went to enquire about transport from the receptionist, while Jocelyn followed Dorian and his grandmother out to the car, in which Dorry was already installed. Esme had obviously decided that she was not a serious rival, and in that she was right. But in the matter of her duties, Dorian was already exacting his due.

Their route was the same as the way to Oban, Dorian declaring that it was one of the finest runs in that part of Scotland, but they turned off before reaching that town, heading for Ballaculish over a long bridge that excited Dorry's interest.

It was a long journey and before they reached Fort William, the child was asleep with his head in Jocelyn's lap, and she was so tired she could not differentiate any more between lochs and mountains; they all began to look alike. Dame Eleanor in the front seat did not seem at all fatigued and continued to ask eager questions, but unlike Jocelyn she had not been awake half the night.

Arrived at the bustling town, which besides being a tourist centre was also a manufacturing place, Jocelyn put Dorry to bed—he was to sleep in her room this time—and went to find Dorian. She wanted to go in search of her family instead of having dinner with him and his grandmother. The hotel manageress had promised to keep an ear open for Dorry, and in any case he was so weary, she felt sure he would not wake.

She found Dorian in the bar waiting for Dame Eleanor, who liked an aperitif before dinner, and he raised his brows when he saw she was still in her travelling clothes.

'Gran will expect you to change for dinner.'

'But I'm not staying.' She told him where she was going and explained about Dorry. He frowned.

'You're not going to walk out on us?'

'That's wasn't my intention, but I ought to give them a look since I'm here.'

'Such filial devotion,' he gibed 'but I don't altogether trust you. Give me the address where they're staying and if you're not back by midnight, I'll come and get you.'

'Don't bother. I'm sure I'm not indispensable.'

'We've been into all that.' He grinned suddenly. 'I might manage Dorry, but I couldn't possibly act as lady's maid to Gran.'

'I prefer that function to acting as your finacée,' she returned. 'It's an easier part.'

'Is it so difficult having to ... er ... tolerate me?' he asked, his eyes glinting dangerously. 'Sit down and let me get you a drink while we discuss it.'

An overture? An indication that she had been forgiven? Or a fresh approach? He was looking supremely attractive, freshly shaved, his face smooth and brown, his dark jacket beautifully tailored to fit his broad shoulders and narrow waist.

'Thanks, but I can't stop,' she said briefly. 'I don't want to be late back.'

'Okay, so long as you do come back. And you will continue to stand in as my fiancée—we may meet a few more McTavishes. Go and revel with your moutaineers, but I want that address first.'

She gave him the name of the modest guest-house where George and Ronald were staying, and went to find them, carefully transferring the ring to her right hand. Dorian had not yet noticed it.

Her family were pleased to see her and told her jubilantly that they had climbed Ben Nevis, though not by the famous north face. Next day they were moving on to essay the Grey Corries. Mrs Seymour had written to say that she was recuperating in the balmy air of Bournemouth and bemoaned their absence. She took the opportunity to point out her own unselfishness in permitting them to indulge in their peculiar choice of recreation; she did not like mountains.

'And I'm sure Jo is bored stiff,' she concluded her

letter, 'and wishing she'd come with me.'

Jocelyn smiled. Whatever else she had been she had not suffered from boredom!

They seemed quite relieved that she did not intend to stay with them; the Grey Corries would absorb them, nor did George raise any objection to her continued association with Dorian Armitage, now that Dame Eleanor had joined the expedition, though he thought his daughter would find the old lady a bit of a handful. He had lively recollections of her domineering ways when he had worked in the theatre where she was appearing.

'Oh, Jo knows what she's doing,' Ronald declared. 'If she can get in with the old dear she may help her to get a job.'

Jocelyn admitted that the thought had crossed her mind, but that was not the reason for waiting upon her.

'She'll forget all about me when she goes back to town,' she said despondently.

Ron was not much interested in Jocelyn's prospects, for he had no sympathy with her ambitions, being certain she would give up the stage and get married as soon as the right man came along, which to his mind was a much more suitable fate for a pretty girl. Reverting to his own hobby, he went on:

'Dad and I hope to go to Skye one year, that's if we can square Mum. There's good climbing in the Cuillins.'

They parted amicably, having arranged that Jocelyn would meet them in Edinburgh in time to take the motorail back to London.

Of her supposed engagement to Dorian, Jocelyn made no mention, and hoped they would never hear about it.

It was a beautiful drive to Mallaig, past lochs and mountains and finally through wooded landscape until the sea was reached. At Glenfinnian on Loch Shiel, Dorian stopped to take Dorry to the top of the round tower that had been erected to commemorate the spot where Prince Charlie had landed before the fatal uprising of '45, while Jocelyn and Dame Eleanor sat in the car waiting for their return.

'They seem to be getting on well together,' the old lady said with satisfaction. 'Pity he let Elise keep them apart.' She looked slyly at Jocelyn 'But I'm always sorry for only children. I hope you'll give him some brothers and sisters.'

Jocelyn hoped she was managing to conceal her consternation, at this plain speaking; Dame Eleanor was going to be disappointed!

Further on a small cairn marked the place where the defeated Prince had left Scottish soil, never to return. Dorian took the opportunity to improve his son's historical knowledge, for Dorry had never heard of Charles Edward Stuart.

They reached Mallaig in time for lunch, which they took at a restuarant, and a very good one it was, after checking in at the hotel. After that they drove the short distance to the harbour, amid a cloud of seagulls. Jocelyn had never seen so many seabirds, they were everywhere, perched on the roofs and covering a tiny island off shore where many of them slept at night so that it looked as if it were covered with snow. That Mallaig possessed a kipper factory was part of its attraction for them, and they always assembled when the catch was landed from the fishing boats. Fishing and tourists were Mallaig's industries. It was a small seaport from which could be seen the isles of Rhum and Eigg with the tips of the Cuillins of Skye visible when it was clear above the headland which masked that island. Sheep were much in evidence; they wandered at will through the little town, cropping the grassy banks which served most of the houses including the hotel for gardens, thus obviating the need to mow them. Dorry was much intrigued by them, though he thought it was poor husbandry to let them roam where ill-intentioned people might steal their fleeces.

'To make the knit,' as he put it, and seeing one ragged-looking ewe, insisted that some fanatical knitter had helped herself to its wool.

His father took him to the end of the quay and he watched round-eyed as the cars were being loaded into the ferry for Skye. He came back full of excitement to describe the operation to the other two, how the lift came up, the cars drove on and were lowered into the hold.

'Dozens and dozens of them!' he declared.

'It must be a big ship,' Jocelyn remarked.

'Not as big as the one that brought me from France. But I want to go on her now. Papa, why must I wait until tomorrow?'

'Because it's too late. We want to spend a whole day there.'

'That's what I came for,' Dame Eleanor reminded them.

But next day the old lady was too exhausted to undertake the trip. Her indomitable spirit had fought against her frailty, but now it had overcome her, and Dorian insisted she must spend a day in bed. She was emphatic that the others must go, but Jocelyn volunteered to stay with her and thought Dorian looked relieved. At dinner upon the previous night he had been exchanging glances with a bold-eyed blonde and later Jocelyn had seen them sitting together in the dimness of the television room, after his grandmother had retired. She had a shrewd idea that the blonde was also going to Skye and would be travelling on the same boat. Dorian's attitude towards herself had been cool and aloof since the night beside Loch Lomond, except for their brief exchange before she had gone to see her people, and she had no wish to allow him to flaunt his new conquest in front of her as he probably intended to do if Dame Eleanor's restraining presence was removed. Let him look after his son while she stayed with her other responsibility—she was not going to provide the opportunity for chasing blondes.'

Dorry had been momentarily dashed, when his father accepted Jocelyn's offer, but soon recovered his spirits after a whispered conversation with him.

'*Alors*, this is an expedition for men,' he said loftily.

Jocelyn recognised Dorian's diplomacy. Blonde or no blonde, he did not want her company any more than she wanted his. She supported him by saying:

'Yes, it's rather strenuous for mere females and I might be sick on the boat.'

'*Moi*, I do not suffer from *mal de mer*,' he told her with a superior air, 'but if you do, it's well that you do not come.'

They went off after breakfast, driving down to the quay amid the usual flock of seagulls. A small red sports car followed them in which was seated the blonde, and Jocelyn hoped she would not spoil Dorry's day, but she rather suspected that Dorian's interest in her was assumed for her benefit and if she were not there he would lose her when they arrived at Armadale.

He had noticed the ring before they left Fort William and drawn her aside to say:

'I'd forgotten that necessary adjunct, but before we leave you must let me buy you something better than that trumpery article.'

'No need to waste your money,' she had returned. 'I prefer to wear my own.'

He had looked at her with veiled eyes and shrugging his shoulders, remarked: 'As you please,' before he walked away from her.

He had not appreciated her gesture, for the cheap

little ring would do him no credit in his grandmother's eyes, if she happened to notice it, and his attentions to the blonde were to pay her out for her independence. She tried to persuade herself that she did not mind whom he chose to favour, but her pride was pricked, which was probably what he had intended. Nor was the fictitious engagement necessary any longer, for the self-engrossed holidaymakers took no interest in them and Dame Eleanor was an effective chaperone. But as she still believed in it, it was too soon to break it off. They were fortunate that nobody recognised the actors, not connecting the famous Dorian Armitage with this family man escorted by an old woman, his small son and the unobtrusive 'governess.'

Dame Eleanor slept all the morning, but in the afternoon she asked Jocelyn to sit with her. She had been rather put out to find the girl had not gone with the others, but Jocelyn assured her that she too was feeling tired. The old lady snorted and told her:

'Modern girls have no stamina.'

Jocelyn found her perusing the script of Dorian's play, which was called *Time-Honoured Lancaster*, a title borrowed from Shakespeare, and though John of Gaunt was under sixty when he died, the Bard indicated that he was an old man. Possibly in an age when life expectancy was so short, he would seem so, but he was represented as still vigorous up to the end in this play.

'Read it to me,' Dame Eleanor commanded, 'my eyes are tired.'

Being very curious about it, Jocelyn was only too pleased to comply.

'Where have you got up to?' she enquired.

'Start at the beginning, please. Plays are meant to be spoken. I shall get a better idea of it if I hear it aloud.'

So throughout the long summer afternoon Jocelyn read, and soon became absorbed in what she was reading. It was a strong, dramatic play, in which Dorian would be superb, and the Plantagenet court at that period was at its most magnificent, so he would also look wonderful in the sumptuous clothing.

'Dorian couldn't have a finer vehicle to show his genius,' Dame Eleanor declared, as she finished it.

'He'll be marvellous,' Jocelyn said fervently.

'That mayn't be enough to ensure success,' Dame Eleanor stated. 'True, *Richard of Bordeaux* wasn't expected to run, but it did. However, that was a good many years ago and the public is unpredicatable. Sensationalism is all the vogue—and people taking their clothes off. I don't know if a good straight play has much chance.'

'But some people still appreciate good acting,' Jocelyn protested.

'Not enough. Still, Dorian has a following and if he gets enough famous names in the cast...' Her voice died away and she lay back on her pillows and closed her eyes. Jocelyn looked at her anxiously.

'I've tired you, madam?'

'No, no, and don't call me madam,' the old lady said peevishly. 'Dame Eleanor will do. You read well, child, you've been blessed with a lovely voice, there's music in it.'

Jocelyn would have been a fool if she had not known she could speak well. She had a natural ear for inflection and a good vocal range, but she was pleased to hear it praised by such a knowledgeable actress.

Dame Eleanor opened her eyes and gave her a keen glance.

'When's the wedding to be?

'The ... what?' Jocelyn asked, startled by the abrupt question.

'Your marriage. I suppose you and Dorian are going to get married?'

Jocelyn hesitated. She hated deceiving the old lady,

but it was largely upon her account that Dorian had insisted upon preserving the myth. Dame Eleanor was watching her expressive face closely, and now she asked:

'Something's wrong, isn't it?'

'Why should you think that?' Jocelyn parried.

'I'm not blind, child. Dorian doesn't act like a man in love and you don't look happy. Have you quarrelled or are you merely having second thoughts? Perhaps you were too impulsive—you hadn't known him long, had you?'

'We were in *The Dream* together,' Jocelyn reminded her, though during that production Dorian had barely noticed her; it was where it had begun for her. Then, weary of pretence, she proceeded to explain the circumstances that had led up to her supposed engagement.

'Dorian must have some regard for you to care what was said about you,' Dame Eleanor said thoughtfully. 'Why don't you try to make a go of it? He only needs a little persuasion, I'm sure, to make it a genuine one. You'd be so good for him. Elise wasn't, she was just a frivolous little doll, and Dorry needs a mother.'

'Dorian doesn't want to marry me,' Jocelyn objected. 'I've a little pride, Dame Eleanor, I couldn't suggest to him that he did.'

The old lady chuckled. 'I thought that in these days of Woman's Lib, girls could do their share of proposing.'

'Well, I can't,' Jocelyn was emphatic. It was an unforseen complication that Dame Eleanor might approve and uphold her claim upon Dorian. 'You ... you won't say anything to him?' she added anxiously. 'He'll be furious that I told you without consulting him.'

'I'm not afraid of Dorian's furies,' Dame Eleanor smiled. 'I'm used to them. A great deal of storm and thunder but no malice underneath. Let me tell you, pride will get you nowhere, child. You've got him, and you're a woman, aren't you? You should be able to hold him.'

'But I haven't got him, he doesn't want me,' Jocelyn cried despairingly.

'Are you sure he doesn't want you?'

Jocelyn's face flamed. 'Not ... honestly,' she murmured.

'Aha, so he's made a pass at you. I'd think less of him if he hadn't. Well then, what's stopping you? Use some guile, girl.'

'Oh, what the use?' Jocelyn sighed. 'I don't want to be the latest addition to his collection of trophies, and that's all I'd be.'

Dame Eleanor looked annoyed by this remark, and Jocelyn realised she had been tactless to be so frank. She was his grandmother.

'Poor Dorian has been much maligned,' the old lady said a little stiffly. 'He's not a fish, of course, and for years he's been tied to that bigoted little Elise who wouldn't set him free, but his affairs have been greatly exaggerated. Now she's dead he needs a real wife, and you'd do very well.'

'He doesn't love me,' Jocelyn told her flatly.

'That's not essential. He's attracted, isn't he, and you're not a soppy schoolgirl. Dorian's past a boy's first romantic passion, and he's learned how misleading that can be. He'll choose more carefully next time. He ought to give Dorry a stepmother and a woman who will appreciate him. Esme was out to get him, and I'm thankful he's had the sense to get shot of that limpet. She doesn't like children, but you do. You'd be very suitable.'

'I don't think I'd want to marry simply to be an unpaid nursemaid,' Jocelyn protested, 'although I'm fond of Dorry. But he'd soon grow away from me when he goes to school.'

'Nevertheless he should have a home to come back to. Have you ever seen Dorian's flat?'

'No, of course not.'

'Very elegant ... and cold. Oh, there are plenty of fires and radiators, but it's too immaculate, too unlived in. His housekeeper—actually she lives in the building and does for him when he's in residence—has no idea of making it look homelike. I think Dorian is often lonely and I don't think Dorry would be happy there as it is.'

This picture of Dorian's abode depressed Jocelyn, but she reflected that he was not at home much.

'I'm sure Dorian isn't domesticated,' she remarked, 'and I did hint that Dorry needed a proper home. He offered me the position of his housekeeper, but of course he wasn't serious.'

Dame Eleanor chuckled. 'Are you sure he wasn't? He's thinking along the right lines, and housekeepers often become wives.'

'But I'm an actress, Dame Eleanor, I'm not sure I want to give up my profession.'

'Yes, and you've considerable talent, but you needn't give up. You can always go back to the stage when Dorry is older. Dorian could help to get you launched and you'd find your personality had been deepened and enriched by more experience of life.'

Exactly what Dorian was always hinting.

'I don't know that I dare hinge my life on Dorian's favours,' Jocelyn said a little bitterly. 'As I said, he doesn't love me, while I...' She hesitated, blushing crimson; it seemed almost impertinence to confess her feelings to this autocratic old lady.

'Love him,' Dame Eleanor finished for her. 'Why be ashamed of it? And why do you try to conceal it?'

'Because it's what Dorian expects of every woman he meets.' Jocelyn's bitterness increased. 'I'm not going to allow him to trample on my heart and then when he's had enough of me, find me a good part as sop.'

'Bravo!' the old lady cried mockingly, her dark eyes sparkling with amusement.

'Well, it's what would happen,' Jocelyn said defensively. She glanced at her companion anxiously. 'You won't give me away?'

'Possibly he's well aware of your feelings.'

'I hope not,' Jocelyn exclaimed fervently. 'I don't think he is.'

Her eyes went to the sunlit scene outside; it was a day of alternate shade and sunshine, clouds drifting from the west, alternately obscuring and revealing the distant Isles. Across the Sleat Dorian and his son were, she hoped, enjoying their day together. Dorry would come rushing back to relate to her all his adventures. He would miss her when they parted. She sighed.

Dame Eleanor was scrutinising her intently, noticing the long slim fingers clasped about her knee, the bare neck and arms tinted a delicate brown by a not too hot sun, her hair loosely knotted behind her well-shaped head, showing golden lights among its auburn coils. The girl had looks and poise, it was not surprising she had caught her grandson's wandering fancy, but she was not happy about it, as was betrayed by the wistful droop of her well shaped mouth with its passionate underlip and the sadness in her clouded blue eyes.

'One thing I can tell you, my girl,' the old lady said sententiously. 'Regret for our sins is nothing compared with what we feel for the opportunities we missed.'

Jocelyn smiled. 'Did you miss any?'

'Precious few, sinful or otherwise, so I've no regrets. I hope you won't have any.'

'I hope I'll never regret having done what was right.' Jocelyn said primly.

'How pi we are!' the old lady laughed. 'Listen to

her!' She addressed the empty room as though she were speaking on stage. 'She's all the things that have gone right out of fashion, honest, virtuous, unvenial and high-principled—qualities all too rare nowadays.'

She was thinking she would have something to say to her grandson. He too was missing an opportunity.

Suspecting mockery, Jocelyn flushed. 'I'm sorry if I appear a prig to you.'

'Far from it. I admire you immensely, but I don't know if you'll get very far. It's the ungodly who flourish like green bay trees. So, when you've jilted Dorian, or he's jilted you, what are you going to do when you get back to London?'

'Trail round the agencies looking for a job,' Jocelyn told her dejectedly.

'Which Dorian could help you to get.'

'I couldn't ask him.' She was emphatic.

'Stiff-necked little idiot. He owes you something.'

'He doesn't owe me anything. Any service I've given to Dorian has been amply repaid by his generosity over my expenses.'

'The least he could do.' Dame Eleanor looked pointedly at the ring on Jocelyn's third finger. 'Was that his idea of an engagement ring?'

'No. I wouldn't let him give me one. This is mine.'

'I thought it didn't look like a gift from Dorian. You should have at least got a diamond out of him.'

'If I had, I should have had to return it, which would have been a waste of money, although of course he could have given it to the next woman in his life.'

'Poor boy, you have got your knife into him.'

'He doesn't care,' Jocelyn said drearily.

Dame Eleanor shifted on her pillows. 'Has it occurred to you that he may misinterpret your independence into dislike of him?'

'It's less dangerous than letting him discover I ... don't dislike him,' Jocelyn told her unhappily.

'H'm.' Dame Eleanor gave her a long penetrating look. Jocelyn suddenly wished she had not been so candid; she had no reason to suppose she could trust the old lady to hold her tongue, only instinct, and that might have misled her.

'I hope your chance will come,' Dame Eleanor said vaguely. 'You might prove to be quite a good actress.' She yawned, seeming to lose interest in the conversation. 'Just shake up my pillows, child, I feel sleepy again.'

'I'm afraid I've tired you,' Jocelyn exclaimed contritely, as she hastened to adjust the bedclothes. 'First reading the play and then all that talk about me. I'm sorry.'

'Don't be,' the old woman murmured drowsily. 'It was most amusing.' Her dark eyes flashed up at the girl with a puckish expression reminiscent of her grandson. 'I haven't been so well entertained for years.' The wrinkled lids closed and she relaxed.

Jocelyn stole out of the room feeling slightly deflated. Dame Eleanor's probings had only been a means of wiling away the ennui of a day in bed. She took no real interest in the fate of Jocelyn Seymour and she had enjoyed the chance to trot out her pet aphorisms. Why should she care? She and Dorian were bright stars high in the theatrical firmament and Jocelyn had not yet risen above the horizon. Perhaps she never would.

She turned the ring on her finger and then took it off. There was no longer any need for that fiction. They had left Mrs McTavish and Esme far behind, Dame Eleanor knew the truth and in this hotel Dorry slept in an alcove in her own room.

Looking at her bare left hand, she wondered if Dorian would notice.

CHAPTER SEVEN

DORIAN and son came back from Skye in high spirits. Dorry had not thought much of the island, which he considered *'triste'*, meaning it was too bleak and bare for his taste, but he had thoroughly enjoyed the crossing both going and coming back.

'Except for the silly lady,' he confided to Jocelyn. 'She treated me like a baby and asked me if I loved my papa. Of course I do, but men don't talk about love.'

'What happened to her when you landed?' Jocelyn asked, smiling at this naïve assertion.

'*Alors*, we left her behind. Her car did not go as fast as ours, but she was there on the boat when we came back and she told Papa he was very ungallant. What does that mean, Mademoiselle Jo?'

'That he shouldn't have left her behind.'

'But we didn't want her with us. Papa said she was another clinging limpet. Limpets stick, don't they? You can't pull them off the rocks. Papa doesn't like limpets and I don't too. She gave me a lot of sweets, but they made me feel ill. *Peut-être* I eat too many.'

Such was Dorry's account of Dorian's blonde. Jocelyn felt a little sorry for her. Dorian's eye-play at dinner had been encouraging, and he must have told her they were also going over to Skye next day. Yet he had ruthlessly discarded her as soon as he landed, preferring the sole company of his small son. She had made the same mistake that Esme had made of being too obviously available, and he had felt no further interest in her. Jocelyn accepted this as an object lesson. If she followed Dame Eleanor's advice and sought to exert a hold over him, he would very soon show her she was not wanted.

After obtaining a light meal for Dorry, she put the boy to bed, for he was very sleepy after a long day in the open air. She wished afterwards that she had shared it with him, for as she changed into her blue dress for dinner she remembered that Dame Eleanor was still in bed and she would be alone with Dorian—as much alone as anyone could be in a room full of people.

However, she had no wish to forgo her dinner, and in all probability he would elect to join his blonde limpet, but when she came into the dining room he was sitting alone at the table that had been allocated to them, apparently waiting for her to join him, for he stood up as she hesitated in the doorway, and pulled out a chair for her.

Because of his late return from Skye he was taking his meal rather later than usual and he had changed into his formal suit, which made him look distinguished among the slovenly garb of the majority of the guests, already half way through their dinner. Looking round at the other men, most of whom were wining and dining a little too well, Jocelyn thought how well groomed and handsome he looked and felt a little stir of pride to be sitting with him.

'Dorry asleep?' he enquired as he took his seat opposite to her.

'Went out like a light. You seem to have exhausted him. All the same, I'll go and have a look at him after dinner.'

'He should be grateful for such devoted service.'

Said with an edge to his voice, which caused her to look at him in surprise, and it caused her a moment's disquiet, as she recalled that while she had been attending to Dorry, he had been to see his grandmother.

He had been with her for some time and it flashed across her mind that Dame Eleanor might have been indiscreet. Hastily she reassured herself; they had had other things to talk about besides her insignificant self. He would have been describing the island, which the old lady's fatigue had defrauded her from visiting.

'Gran says you read the whole of *Time-Honoured Lancaster* to her,' he went on, with the same slight edge. 'That was a noble feat.' Then his enthusiasm for the play conquered whatever was needling him and he asked eagerly: 'What did you think of it?'

'It was quite gripping in places, and you'll be marvellous in it,' she told him with shining eyes.

'Thank you. I recall you originally introduced yourself as one of my fans,' he said drily, 'but I hope my performance will have a more artistic appeal than to cater for the romantic susceptibilities of hysterical young females.'

Definitely something had displeased him.

'You shouldn't despise them,' she reproached him, wondering if he considered she was one of them. 'Their money is as good as anybody else's, even if they are more interested in the man than the play.'

'Naturally you would consider the commercial angle is the more important,' he said disagreeably.

'Isn't that what fills the theatre?' she pointed out, determined not to take offence.

They discussed the play while the waitress brought their food, and the subject lasted through the soup and fish—small fried mackerel freshly caught, the hotel served four courses. The puzzling undercurrent vanished from Dorian's voice while he outlined the company's plans for the production, and she listened with wrapt attention. For once they seemed entirely en rapport.

As she placed her knife and fork together having finished the fish, his eyes suddenly narrowed. He broke off what he was saying, and his hand shot across the table to grasp her left wrist, and he looked up accusingly from her bare fingers into her face.

'Why did you take it off?'

'There's no longer any need to wear it. Our little act was only retained for your grandmother's benefit, wasn't it? This afternoon I told her the truth.'

'Sure it was the truth?' he asked ominously. 'She seemed under the impression that you still had some claim upon me. I would rather you'd consulted me before you confided in her.'

He released her wrist and sat back in his chair, regarding her with a queer glitter in his eyes.

'If I'd done, as I ought to have done, bought you a diamond, you wouldn't have been so ready to discard it ... no, not a diamond, but sapphires, dark ones, like your eyes. You've got beautiful eyes, Jocelyn, an unusual colour and so expressive ... an asset for an actress, and you're quite a clever little actress, aren't you, my girl, with your deceptive innocent air. No one, especially a mere man would dream you were so ... calculating.'

He spat out the last word and Jocelyn stared at him in bewilderment.

'What on earth's got into you, Dorian?' she asked. 'I don't want jewels, least of all from you. I took the ring off because there was no point in wearing it any longer.'

'That does surprise me. From your point of view, I should have thought there was a great deal of point in continuing to wear it.'

'No, it would be deceitful, and I don't like pretence.'

'Don't you, my girl? It seems to me you make a fine art of it. You certainly managed Gran very subtly.'

The waitress came with the next course, setting a plate of lamb cutlets in front of them, and Jocelyn stared at them unseeingly wincing from Dorian's cold contempt. Dame Eleanor must have said something to so incense him, but what? She strove to recall all that had passed between them. Prominent had been the old woman's insistence that she should take advantage of her position to induce Dorian to marry her. An awful conviction grew in her mind that Dame Eleanor had been trying to play providence to bring about that desired culmination, with the result that Dorian believed she had sought to enlist his grandmother's aid to support her. His next words seemed to confirm this supposition. He waited until the vegetables had been served and the waitress had retreated, then he said sarcastically:

'Such a noble little woman, so unselfish, giving up a whole day of her holiday to devote herself to a tired old lady, and such an opportunity for a long cosy chat. Poor little orphan Dorry, longing for a mother, the reprehensible actor needing the reforming influence of a good wife and the comforts of a settled home, and who could be a better candidate to achieve all these excellent things than the so virtuous, so self-sacrificing Jocelyn Seymour?'

Colour flooded Jocelyn's pale cheeks and her eyes widened in dismay at this monstrous distortion of her naïve confidences. How could she have been such a fool to trust Dame Eleanor? The old lady had entirely misrepresented her.

'Dorian, I never said ... I never meant ... Oh, how could she!' She choked, covering her mouth with her table napkin while she gazed at him with anguished eyes.

Dorian shrugged his shoulders and went on eating his dinner, regardless of her distress.

'I can recommend these cutlets,' he announced appreciatively. 'They're better than anything we've been served so far. Don't let yours grow cold.'

'I don't care if they freeze,' she cried passionately. 'Food would choke me...'

'You seem a little overcome,' he agreed, 'but it's a pity to waste an appetising dish because you've permitted your ill temper to affect your appetite.'

Maddeningly, irritatingly calm, but with a glint in his eyes that showed he was deliberately baiting her.

'Temper!' she exclaimed with a half sob. 'Please tell me what Dame Eleanor said to you.'

'Ah, that would be a breach of confidence. Strange as it may seem, in spite of my disastrous marriage to Elise, of which she never approved, she's very anxious to set the noose of matrimony about my neck once more. She, like you, wants to see me tamed into a domestic pet, I'll admit she has some reason on her side, especially with regard to Dorry. He's been your trump card, hasn't he, and you've played him very successfully. I was completely taken in, in fact I was pleased and touched by your devotion to him, but now I understand it was all an act. Very enterprising, if dishonest.'

He was outwardly cold, face and voice expressing no more emotion than the potato he was eating. Jocelyn could sense that underneath his calm, he was furiously angry, the glitter in his green-gold eyes betrayed him. His unjust accusation of self-interest regarding Dorry fired her own temper, and she told him fiercely:

'Whatever I said to Dame Eleanor was also spoken in confidence, but she doesn't seem to have had your scruples about disclosing it. Perhaps she meant well, and between you you've twisted my meaning out of all recognition, but I won't allow you to attribute base motives to my affection for Dorry, that's genuine and sincere. I *am* very fond of the boy and it's for his sake I've put up with your insulting behaviour...'

'Insulting?' he interrupted quickly. 'I've never tried to insult you.'

'Some of your ... er ... advances could be considered so.'

His eyes flashed green fire. 'Most women regard my attentions as a compliment, and I can't say you seemed particularly averse to them, though you did play hard to get. You had your reasons for that, you hoped to enveigle me into a proposal. But I'm too old a bird to allow my heart to rule my head; I shall only consider marriage after carefully weighing up the pros and cons. I will admit that at Oban ...'

He broke off, and his face softened a little.

Jocelyn recalled the memory of that golden midsummer day with nostalgic yearning. She had been happy then, they had all been happy together, and during the following expeditions, Dorian's attempts at a flirtation had merely added spice to their friendship, until the night by Loch Lomond.

'We had such lovely days out,' she said softly. 'Why did you have to spoil everything?'

'It was inevitable,' he told her more gently. 'Human relationships can't stay static, especially where a man's feelings are involved.'

She flashed him a scornful look.

'I didn't know you had any, only urges.'

He blinked. 'Charming!' he exclaimed.

'Not the word I should choose.'

'Perhaps not. Well, I'll concede I've misjudged you about Dorry. I believe you do care for the child, however much you despise his father.'

'I don't despise you, Dorian, but ...'

'No? Possibly my assets make up for my deficiencies of character.'

Jocelyn felt she could endure no more of this verbal warfare. Each was trying to wound the other and he was succeeding, though she fancied one or two of her shafts had gone home.

'Oh, can't we forget it all?' she asked desperately.

'We've only one more day here, so please let's spend it amicably, even if I have displeased you by exploding the myth of our engagement.'

For that seemed to be the source of his grievance.

'About that, I've something to say to you.'

She looked at him questioningly, but at that moment the waitress came to remove their plates and serve the dessert. For her benefit, Dorian made some impersonal remarks about the Island of Skye, and Jocelyn murmured mechanical replies, puzzled by his demeanour. Anger had given place to a kind of suppressed amusement and his eyes were sardonic. She knew how perverse his humour could be and dreaded his next assault. She refused the sweet, but Dorian helped himself to the cheese board. Temper had not impaired his appetite.

When the waitress had gone, he said pensively:

'My grandmother was very persuasive. The picture she drew of my austere flat, my cold lonely life, positively made me shiver, and her account of poor Dorry being bullied at a boarding school was bloodcurdling. She still thinks they haven't improved upon Tom Brown. So would you consider making our fake engagement a reality?'

This was the last thing she had expected him to say. She stared at him blankly, unable to believe her ears. He could not be seriously proposing to her, not after all the nasty things he had said.

'You must be joking,' she said feebly.

'I'm perfectly serious, but perhaps I should explain that I'm only offering you a marriage of convenience. My flat is quite spacious, there are two bedrooms and a box room for Dorry. My present help will, I'm sure be pleased to continue to do the housework. Dorry can go to a nearby day school, my engagements will frequently take me away from home—for instance I'll be several weeks in Manchester if we decide to try out

Time-Honoured Lancaster there. I'll give you an adequate allowance for housekeeping and for your personal use. You'll be welcome to entertain your friends and relations, preferably when I'm not there, and I'll expect you to entertain mine when I am. That's the proposition. Think it over.'

He addressed himself to his cheese and biscuits.

Jocelyn's initial surprise faded before growing resentment. His cold considered words were so many blows upon her heart. There was no hint or suggestion of any personal feeling. The collected businesslike person opposite to her bore no relation to the passionate man who had so stirred her by Loch Lomond. She said a little tartly:

'Do you imagine you can live on platonic terms with a woman?'

'Of course I can if I want to. I'm not so undisciplined as you seem to imagine. Oh, I know what's troubling your frigid little soul, but that's all over, you froze it to death. You need not be afraid of any more demonstrations from me.'

'Then what will you get out of it?' she asked bluntly.

'A well run flat, I hope, you're not incompetent, but it's for Dorry's sake I'm proposing to make you his stepmother. As has been so often reiterated, he needs a home.'

'I see.' She would be little more than a glorified housekeeper, the position he had once offered her in jest and she had declared was an impossibility. It would be possible if she were protected by his name, but that was all he meant to give her. She looked at him uncertainly. Intuitively she felt that his controlled manner concealed some inner conflict, and that he was secretly motivated by strong emotion, but what that was she could not conceive. It might be anger, hate, lust or vindictiveness, but not, she was sure, love.

If she became his wife, she would find out, and perhaps to her cost.

'And my career?' she asked.

'Of course you'd have to give that up, but you haven't got very far with it, have you?'

That hurt her, though it was true, but he himself had had to start in a humble way when no younger than herself. He regarded her ambitions of no importance, but she would only contemplate giving up the stage for someone who returned her love, which he had definitely indicated he did not. Even his brief fancy for her had died, he had told her. That left Dorry to be considered, but it would be a big sacrifice to make, even for him.

'Was this Dame Eleanor's suggestion?' she asked.

'Not entirely. Oh, she did tell me that you were a pearl beyond price and I'd be a fool to let you slip through my fingers. Such a paragon of all the virtues! But paragons make me freeze; however, we know you consider I'm damaged goods, so that won't distress you. You'll get no contaminating caresses from me.'

Jocelyn shrank inwardly from the ice in his face and voice. He was continuing to emphasise that he had proposed out of expediency and had no tenderness for her at all.

The waitress came to clear away their plates, though Jocelyn's was empty. Dorian beckoned to the wine waiter and ordered a bottle of wine.

'To celebrate our betrothal,' he said, but she did not heed him. She was mulling over his disclosures. Dame Eleanor had obviously urged him to marry her, pointing out the advantages of having a home-maker for Dorry and himself, but she did not know all that had passed between them. Dorian could not forget the rebuff she had given him by Loch Lomond; her words still rankled. In time he might forgive her, might also come to be reconciled to her. She would be there, in his home, and his grandmother believed that if she were clever, she could win him in the end. But she must give up her hope of a stage career, and she might never succeed in breaking down his antagonism. Nor did she deceive herself that he would be faithful to her. The nature of their union would provide him with an excuse to seek other diversions, and that would be humiliating. As for Dorry, he would as time went by become less and less dependent upon her. Moreover, he was very sensitive and would soon come to realise that the two people he loved were estranged, as his real mother had been from his father, and that would not make for his happiness.

The wine waiter brought the drink and poured some out for Dorian's approval. He sipped, nodded and the man filled their glasses. When he had gone, Dorian raised his with a mocking smile:

'To my maiden bride, the untouchable paragon.'

Jocelyn restrained an impulse to throw her wine into his jeering face. She had an unpleasant suspicion that his grandmother had also betrayed that she loved him, and this dig would be but the first of many. He knew only too well how to wound her.

'You're perfectly hateful, Dorian,' she burst out. 'And nothing would induce me to marry you on the terms you've specified.'

Sheer astonishment showed in his face, he had been so certain that she would accept him.

'Not even Dorry?' he queried.

'No, not even Dorry. It wouldn't work. He thinks a lot of you, Dorian, and if you're always going away, if you treat me like dirt, he won't be happy.'

'My dear girl, how you exaggerate! I'd never treat you like dirt. You're much too immaculate and superior. Rather I'd set you on a pedestal and offer you my profound respect.'

'Who wants that?' she muttered savagely, and saw

unmistakable triumph in his eyes. Unable to endure further baiting, she got to her feet. 'I don't want any more of your beastly sarcasm, Dorian. I'm going to bed.'

'Sit down, you little idiot!' He spoke so fiercely that she obeyed automatically. 'Must you make a spectacle of yourself in front of the whole room? Drink your wine and calm down.' She saw heads were turning in their direction and with an effort tried to look unconcerned, hastily drinking her wine. Dorian was watching her with amused complacency, and she sensed he was pleased that he had been able to provoke her to such fury. She wished she had been able to appear more dignified. Her eyes burned with sullen resentment, and she learned then that love could turn to hate.

'So I'm to take it that my offer is declined without thanks?' he enquired, wiping his mouth with his table napkin.

'You're so right,' she told him, with assumed sweetness. 'And I shan't even ask you to look upon me as a sister, which I believe is the traditional sop offered to a rejected suitor.'

He laughed, and some of the tension between them evaporated.

'Never having had a sister I don't know how I'd feel towards one—not, I'm sure, as I feel towards you.' He gave her an odd look.

'Have you any feelings towards me? she asked eagerly, 'other than ... than respect?'

He took so long to answer that her heartbeats quickened. If he confessed he still desired her it would make all the difference. Deliberately he poured himself another glass of wine and drank it. Then he said:

'Only complete indifference. Incidentally, tomorrow I'm taking Gran and Dorry down to Arisaig. Dorry wants to play on the white sands. Since our relations are a little strained, perhaps you'd feel more comfortable if you developed a headache and stayed behind.'

'Another deception?' she asked, smiling wanly to disguise her intense chagrin.

'Deception? It wouldn't amount to that, merely another act. All the world's a stage and the only one where you can display your talents until you've been able to impress some management with their worth, and another singing fairy comes your way.'

'I'm not really a singer,' she began.

'Not really anything, are you? I'm afraid there are no ingenues in *Time-Honoured Lancaster*.'

'I never thought of that.' But she had though she had not aspired to anything beyond a walk-on. He was cruel to deride her lack of success.

'Didn't you?' he said indifferently. 'But we're wandering from the point.' He eyed her downcast face with a satirical twist of his lips. 'A headache is a commonplace excuse. No one can dispute its validity. You see, Elise educated me in all the feminine evasive tactics.'

Elise again. She must remember his first wife had poisoned him against her sex and be charitable.

Tomorrow was to be their last day in the Highlands and he was determined not to spend it in her company. She sighed, for though it was as well their holiday was ending and she would see no more of Dorian, the parting with Dorry would be a wrench.

'Very well,' she said tonelessly. 'A headache it shall be, in fact I've the beginnings of one now. May I go, please?'

'You're free to do exactly as you like.'

She stood up. 'Well then, goodnight.'

'Goodnight.' He turned away from her and his hand went towards the bottle of wine.

At the door she glanced back and saw he was watching her through narrowed eyes with an enigmatical smile. The dining room faded into another scene, an illuminated garden, and his face changed into that of a faun with exaggerated make-up elongating his eyes, emphasising their vindictive glitter, while the words she had heard him say for so many nights during *The Dream* rang in her ears:

...'Thou shalt not from this grove,
Till I torment thee for this injury.'

That was what he had been trying to do, torment her because she had again rejected him. But he could not have expected her to agree to his preposterous proposal, nor have really wanted her to. He had made it at his grandmother's instigation, to satisfy the old lady and humiliate herself, and had deliberately couched it in unacceptable terms because he suspected that she loved him and he did not want her love.

The brief illusion faded as the door cut him off from her sight, and she went through into the vestibule.

Strange, unpredictable creature, possessing that inhuman quality that Elise had instilled in him and Aubrey Oliphant had exploited so successfully. She must forget him, but she had cherished his image for so long in her heart it would be a long time before she could eradicate it.

Jocelyn woke next morning feeling so wretched that there was no need of any pretence. When Dorry bounded across to her from his bed in the alcove, she told him she did not feel well enough to get up. He expressed a fleeting sympathy but was far too excited by his father's promise to teach him to swim to be much concerned. He dressed under her direction and paid an unwilling visit to the bathroom. Like all small boys he thought soap and water were unnecessary adjuncts to living, and since he had had a bath the night before, a morning wash was an imposition. She requested that he would ask for some tea and toast to be sent up to her, and after kissing her, he departed full of importance for being entrusted with such an errand.

'I will tell the *garçon* to come quickly,' he told her, and banged the door behind him, causing her head to throb.

Once she was alone, her resolution wavered; it was hard to have to part with the child, but Dorry would grow up, childhood was so short a period, and she would be left bound in a marriage that was not a marriage at all to his unpredictable father who was quite capable of making it into a martyrdom.

The tea and toast arrived and shortly afterwards Dame Eleanor appeared, dressed incongruously for the beach in velvet trousers and her cloak.

'So you're deserting us,' she remarked, her keen eyes studying the girl's pale face. 'You don't look very grand. Ah well, I suppose I'll have to try to remember how to build sandcastles for Dorry's benefit.'

Dorry had overcome his awe of his great-grandmother and they were now excellent friends.

'I was quite a dab at them when I was a child,' she added.

Jocelyn found it difficult to imagine this eminent woman with her hawk-like features as a child playing on the sands.

'So you've refused my grandson?' she went on, thereby disclosing that she had been privy to Dorian's proposal. 'No second thoughts?'

Jocelyn smiled wanly. 'No, I'll stick to my profession.'

She wondered if the older woman knew the almost insulting terms which Dorian had offered to her, but it was unlikely, and even Dorian could not have had the audacity to tell his grandmother he loved her.

Dame Eleanor sighed. 'Pity, but you know you own business best. It won't hurt Dorian to discover he isn't invincible, but I hope Esme doesn't get him on the rebound.'

Dorry came rushing in, demanding to know if she were coming.

'In a minute,' his great-grandmother told him. 'And don't make such a noise. Jocelyn's sick.'

'I hope your *mal à la tête* will soon be better,' Dorry said, and kissed her perfunctorily. As he ran out of the door, Dame Eleanor observed:

'He's too young to pretend sympathy with female ailments, but all men find them tiresome, though they may try to disguise it.'

With which profundity, she departed.

As soon as she was sure they would have left, Jocelyn got up. She intended to go out and walk, for the fresh air would revive her and if she could tire herself out fatigue would dull the pain in her heart.

She bought rolls and cheese at the store in Mallaig and went as far as Loch Morar to the south of the town. This was the deepest and one of the most beautiful lochs in the whole country. She wandered along its shores absorbing its quiet and loveliness, for the road came to an end and there were no more cars to disturb her as she strolled along the footpath, though she met occasional campers.

She had tea in Mallaig so that she need not appear for dinner, she could not bear to face Dorian across that table again. After she had put Dorry to bed she did not leave her room. She sat beside him for a long while after he was asleep, black head burrowed into the pillow with only one brown cheek visible. He had brought her back some shells which he had picked up on the beach. She would always treasure them. He was already growing very like his father, but she hoped he would develop a softer, kinder character. She would have no part in moulding it, and if Dorian did marry again, she prayed it would be a woman who would love his son.

The morning departure was too much of a rush for prolonged leavetakings. Jocelyn wanted to catch an early train as she had a long roundabout journey before her, via Glasgow, and the others were going inland to break their journey for a night en route. They would be travelling back to London the day after she had left with George and Ronald from Edinburgh.

Dorry clung to her at parting. Dame Eleanor shook her hand, remarking that she would probably run across her again as the theatrical circle was not very large. Dorian watched them with a sardonic smile.

His grandmother insisted that he must run Jocelyn the short distance to the station, as her case was too heavy for her to carry, in spite of her protests. Impatiently he exclaimed:

'Oh, come along, it won't take a minute.'

He put her into the rear seat of the car without another word. Still in silence he carried her case on to the platform and then said coolly:

'Thanks for all you've done for Dorry, Miss Seymour. A pleasant journey, goodbye,' and strode away before she could speak.

Jocelyn watched the slim, lithe figure disappearing through a blur of tears. The seagulls circled over the station and the train uttering their harsh, discordant cries, as she took her seat. The sea was blue and calm in the early morning sunlight, Eigg and Rhum clearly discernible. As the train pulled out, she could see the hotel and the figures on its terrace, one small one, that might be Dorry.

Dorian had gone, implacable and unforgiving, but what had hurt her most was his deliberate use of her surname.

CHAPTER EIGHT

JOCELYN obtained an engagement in a variety show at a seaside resort for the end of July and August. She got it on the strength of her singing and because the original soubrette had been suddenly taken ill. It was not the sort of work that she liked, but there was nothing else available and she was glad of a chance to get away from London, which seemed unbearably stuffy after the lovely air of the Highlands. Ironically it was another singing part, and she had told Dorian she was not a singer.

She read the theatrical papers assiduoulsy, seeking for news of Dorian, despising herself for her weakness while she did it, but there was none. She did come across a picture of Esme Carr in one of the glossies with the information that she would be starring in a new production in the autumn, but it did not say what it was. Since *Time-Honoured Lancaster* was due in the autumn, Jocelyn wondered if Aubrey Oliphant had been prevailed upon to engage her in spite of Dorian's opposition. It was painful to her to imagine Esme's trivial personality and thin voice in the fine part of Catherine Swynford, but she supposed she would be adequate to support Dorian, whose performance would eclipse anybody else's.

She returned to London during pouring wet weather at the beginning of September. A walk down Shaftesbury Avenue revealed the Paragon Theatre plastered with notices proclaiming 'Last Weeks.' So the management was taking off the musical to accommodate the Plantagenet play. Depressed by the rain and an unrewarding visit to her agent, her heart lifted at the prospect of seeing Dorian on stage. As soon as the advance booking was advertised she would secure a seat for the first night. He would be very different from Oberon as the stately Plantagenet prince, third son of a king, and she assured herself that her interest was purely artistic, though she knew very well it was much more personal.

Then, to her astonishment, she received a letter asking her to come to the Paragon for an audition. It was all the more mystifying because she could not imagine how the management had got hold of her name. Dorian, she was certain, would not have recommended her. He had told her with that nasty glint in his eyes that there were no ingenues in his play and he did not consider she was mature enough to play anything else. The only explanation seemed to be that her agent had learned that extras were needed for crowd work and had sent in her name knowing she was free without waiting to consult her. At first she debated whether she would go, but the desire to see Dorian's theatre and Dorian's colleagues proved too strong for her. She probably would not be engaged anyway and she was unlikely to encounter Dorian himself, for he would not be concerned in the hiring of extras.

She arrived at the stage door in mackintosh and head-scarf, for it was still raining, and was surprised to find she was the only applicant. She wondered if she had mistaken the day or the hour, and fumbled for the letter in her bag as she confronted the doorkeeper, but he was expecting her.

'Miss Seymour?' he asked gruffly. 'Will you come this way, miss.'

He showed her through the pass door down into the stalls. The auditorium was darkened so she could not see if anyone else were there. A solitary spotlight lit the stage which was set with the exotic scenery of the musical.

Jocelyn took off her mac and scarf and sought to tidy her hair with the help of her handbag mirror, leaning forward to catch a gleam of light from the stage. A couple of electricians were working above it upon an overhead batten. She waited a long time and was beginning to think she had been forgotten when a man in dirty slacks and a pullover, carrying a script, walked on to the stage and shielding his eyes with his hand, peered down at her.

'Is Miss Seymour there?'

She stood up. 'Yes, I'm here.'

'Will you come up on to the stage, please?'

She fumbled her way to the pass door and as she went she became aware that some people were sitting at the back of the stalls. She heard a cough and caught the red gleam of a lighted cigarette.

The man on the stage, he was the assistant stage manager, handed her the script of *Time-Honoured Lancaster* open at a page about half way through.

'Will you read from there, darling,' he said—the endearment was quite mechanical. 'I'll give you the cues.'

'Which part?' she asked, glancing at the page.

To her astonishment, he told her: 'Catherine, of course.'

She remembered it from the reading to Dame Eleanor. It was a beautiful and impassioned scene between Catherine and her lover, John, in which he told her he had decided for reasons of policy to marry the heiress to the Spanish throne. They were at that time both widowed, and though he assured her the union would make no difference to their love and she would continue to act as governess to his daughters, Catherine was beset with doubts and despair at the prospect of his remarriage.

Why she was being asked to read the leading female part, which must have been cast ages ago, she could not surmise, nor was it easy to do it, and herself, justice in an empty theatre with the shabby man seated at a card table on the prompt side casually throwing lines at her and the electricians working above her head. But she was not a novice to be easily discomposed, and as the words she was speaking began to grip her, she forgot her surroundings, seeing in her mind's eye the tapestried mediaeval room, the impressive figure of John, Duke of Lancaster, who was also Dorian whom she loved, and in the play, loved her but was divided from her by the great gulf of their respective stations.

She reached the end of the scene and came back to reality. Down in the stalls someone clapped, and then a tall figure came down the gangway and beckoned to her. It was Dame Eleanor.

As in a dream, Jocelyn handed the book to the A.S.M. and went back into the auditorium. Dame Eleanor had been joined by a tall, thin man with scanty red hair and an untidy beard. She recognised Aubrey Oliphant. He was tugging at his beard, as Jocelyn joined them, a trick she remembered from his production of *The Dream* which indicated that he was thinking.

'You read that quite beautifully, dear,' Dame Eleanor said in her deep, resonant voice. 'Aubrey, you've got to do something for this child.'

'My dear lady. I'm a business man, not a philanthropic society,' Aubrey complained. 'The girl is talented, yes, but ...' He shrugged his shoulders expressively.

'You promised,' Dame Eleanor murmured. 'And since I've put my little all into your production, don't I have some say-so as a shareholder?'

Jocelyn understood then how it was she had been

asked to come, and felt a wave of gratitude towards her benefactress, less because she had obtained this interview for her than because she had not forgotten her.

Aubrey proceeded to fire a barrage of questions at her. What had Jocelyn been doing, what parts had she played, what salary had she been paid, when was she free? When she mentioned, somewhat unwilling, that her last engagement had been with a variety show, he suddenly beamed.

'Why, of course, I remember you. You were the singing fairy in *The Dream*.' He hummed vaguely, 'You spotted snakes, with double tongue,' and broke off to continue. 'Very charming you were too. Of course, this play is already in rehearsal. We've decided to cut out the trial run in the provinces, and will open here within a few weeks. It so happens we've had a little contretemps. The young lady we engaged to be Catherine's understudy has suddenly revealed that she's pregnant. Dame Eleanor assured me that you would be suitable for the part, so I agreed to audition you. You will also walk on as a court lady. That will give you practice in wearing the costume and getting the feel of the period, should you ever have to play the part.'

He went on to mention terms, salary and so forth, while Jocelyn gaped at him.

'Do you mean I'm engaged?' she faltered when he stopped.

'Of course, of course, didn't I say so? Your contract will be drawn up and sent to you to sign. But there's one point I must emphasise. Most understudies consider that once their principal is in the theatre apparently hale and hearty they can wander off. You must stay until the end of every performance. Understood?'

'Yes,' Jocelyn said faintly, not understanding at all.

'Good girl. Now if you'll excuse me, Dame Eleanor, I must be off.' He inclined his head towards the older woman. 'I'm a busy man, you know...'

Jocelyn was beginning, 'But, Mr Oliphant...' for she had suddenly realised all that was entailed. She would be in the same company as Dorian and she did not know how he could react to her reappearance. She wanted time to consider and that had not been granted to her.

'Ssh!' Dame Eleaonor gave her a warning look. 'It's all right, Aubrey,' as he glanced at them enquiringly. 'Jocelyn and I are going for a cup of coffee. She's delighted, of course.'

The director strode up the gangway and vanished into the shadows. Dame Eleanor laid her hand upon Jocelyn's arm.

'Weren't going to make stipulations, were you? He wouldn't stand for that.'

'No, but...' Again she was interrupted.

'Let's go and get that coffee. Empty theatres are like mausoleums.'

Over coffee, Jocelyn enquired about Dorry.

'Oh, he's living with me,' the old lady told her. 'He's started day school. You must come and see him. I've a flat in Hampstead, you know, and my maid-cum-everything else adores him. He says she's like Nounou, she's partly French, and they get on like a house on fire. Dorian comes to see him on Sundays—he hasn't much time on other days. I haven't had so much of my grandson's company for years.'

Jocelyn suppressed a little stab of jealousy. All three were getting along splendidly without her, and Dame Eleanor was looking younger and less frail. Dorry had given her a new interest in life. What a good thing she had not accepted Dorian's offer, Jocelyn thought drearily, but she had never anticipated that Dame Eleanor would take over the boy.

Her thoughts reverted to the play. 'So the idea of opening in Manchester was dropped?'

'Yes, such a comfort Dorian won't be going away.'

'Is Esme Carr playing Catherine?' Jocelyn asked for if she were, she did not feel she could sign that contract, even though she would deeply offend her kind benefactress. Esme would make life sheer hell for her understudy.

'No, of course not. Oh, she's in it, she's Blanche of Lancaster, the first duchess, but she only appears in the first act, where she has several scenes with you, but she dies in the last one, which should give you some satisfaction.' The old lady chuckled. She knew there was no love lost between the two actresses.

'But I'm only to be the understudy,' Jocelyn reminded her. 'It's unlikely I'll ever get a chance to play the part.'

'Don't you know who is playing it?'

Jocelyn shook her head.

'Melisande Everett.'

Jocelyn stared. Melisande Everett was beautiful, talented, and had started upon a great career. She had seen her act in a revival of 'Mary Rose', and she had a fey quality, with lovely, wild eyes and a mass of black hair. But Melisande had a terrible weakness, and though her name could still draw, she had been sliding down the theatrical firmament damned with the fatal label, 'unreliable.'

'But is she Dor ... Mr Oliphant's idea of Catherine?' Jocelyn asked, for she thought Melisande too ethereal.

'Trouble was they couldn't find their ideal. Dorian wouldn't have Esme at any price—said he'd walk out if she were engaged for it. So I suggested Melisande, Dorian's got a soft spot for her, and as I said, I'm a shareholder in Aubrey's company, so I've got a right to be considered. I swore she was reformed and pointed out that she's still famous. Actually the poor girl's doomed, she's a near-alcoholic.'

'Then why ...?'

'I'm coming to that. Dorian told me in Scotland that you had the voice, face and figure for the part, but you were too immature and of course unknown. Both those faults can be remedied, so I persuaded Aubrey to audition you for the understudy. Believe me, he was impressed, and you seem to have grown up a bit more since I last saw you. Well, so far Melisande's been exemplary, but sooner or later she'll go on a jag, and then, my dear, you'll get your chance.'

'You devious old lady!' Jocelyn exclaimed, slightly shocked.

Dame Eleanor grinned delightedly. 'I'm still a power to be reckoned with.' She sighed. 'I don't make many public appearances nowadays, I can't remember lines, but I get some fun out of pulling wires. Ever since you read that play to me I was determined you should one day play it. Aubrey's uneasy about Melisande, that's why he insists you must stay in the theatre all the while she's on stage. He knows as well as I do that your day will come.'

'But Dorian——' Jocelyn began. She recalled that Dame Eleanor had said he had a soft spot for her principal. 'Won't he be upset if Miss Everett ... fails? Will he mind me being in the show?'

'He puts the play first,' Dame Eleanor said a little sternly. 'Whatever he feels about Melisande, and I hope she's only one of his fancies, he knows the play must go on and you'll be adequate. You can't get big names to understudy. Whatever silly squabble you and he have had won't influence him where essentials are concerned. If only you hadn't appeared so young and naïve you'd have got the part in the first place, whatever Aubrey said. Why on earth didn't you have an affair with Dorian? That would have ripened you fast enough.'

Jocelyn flushed at this blunt speaking, but she made no rejoinder. Dame Eleanor's words were illuminating, explaining the real motive behind Dorian's desire to 'educate' her. It threw light upon many of his utterances, but it seemed horribly cold-blooded to contemplate seducing her to fit her for a part in a play, but it was typical of the man, an utter ruthlessness to achieve his object. But there were inconsistencies in his conduct and she voiced one of them.

'He said if I married him I must give up the stage.'

'He's not interested in your subsequent career beyond Catherine,' Dame Eleanor told her drily. 'Having decided he couldn't risk giving you the part, he was thinking of his creature comforts. Actresses make poor housekeepers.'

Jocelyn choked back her rising indignation. Not once had Dorian ever considered her feelings or given a thought to her happiness.

He had sought to manipulate her for his own ends, and in that he resembled his grandmother, for she had said she enjoyed pulling strings; human beings seemed to be mere puppets to both of them. In the present situation this proclivity had worked to her advantage. Doubts and scruples vanished before a sudden surge of ambition. If she ever did play the part she would make a success of it, in spite of her youth and naïveté, but the latter was shrinking. Unrequited love was as much an experience as fulfilment, and she sensed a new strength flowing through her. Deep in her innermost heart she had an unshakable belief in her histrionic ability, without which she could never have persevered in the face of continual discouragement. Her mother had often urged her to change to a more certain occupation, but Jocelyn had steadfastly refused.

Given the opportunity she would match Dorian in power and splendour, and thanks to Dame Eleanor's machinations, it seemed that chance might come There were many hazards to frustrate her—the play might not run, Melisande might be completely cured, but she was prepared to face them.

'Thank you, Dame Eleanor, for your faith in me,' she said sincerely, 'and all you've done for me. If the chance comes I shan't fail you.'

Jocelyn sat in the stalls throughout the rehearsals, marking and inwardly digesting, except for her brief appearance among a crowd of others in a court scene. She walked through several understudy rehearsals which were held elsewhere, lethargic affairs under the guidance of the stage manager. Her opposite number Gordon Thomas, an excitable Welshman, did not exert himself, but spoke his lines with ill-concealed boredom.

'You see, I'll never play it,' he told Jocelyn. 'If Dorian should be off, they'd close the theatre. He's irreplaceable.'

She had half longed for, half dreaded her first meeting with Dorian. He must know that she was there. He came to work in a black polo-necked sweater and pants, looking long, lean and dangerous. He was on stage most of the time and when he was not, he sat with Aubrey. He had noticed her on her first morning, soon after she arrived, and gave her a brief nod. And that was all.

He was assiduous in his attentions to Melisande. Often they went out to lunch together during the short midday break. There was a tender protectiveness in his attitude towards her, as if he were anxious she should not fail, which was something Jocelyn had not seen in him before. Melisande wore trousers and a sweater too, which outlined her tall, willowy figure. She was very lovely, with her Irish colouring and an elfin look, which Aubrey decried.

'Try to look a little more earthy, darling,' he told her more than once.

Esme was piqued by Dorian's attentions to her, Jocelyn overheard her telling the sallow Spanish woman, who was playing Constanza of Castile, who was not reputed to be glamorous.

'Dor always says he likes to be a little in love with his leading lady, but it doesn't mean a thing. He was mad about me when I played Titania to his Oberon.'

Which had seemed to be true at the time.

Dorian's heart was very accommodating, Jocelyn thought wryly; he seemed able to direct it in any direction that suited him, but of course it was never seriously involved. She wondered for the hundredth time if he had really loved Elise and if it was her desertion that had made him impervious to any genuine feeling.

The dress rehearsal was terribly long and tedious, with hours spent adjusting the lighting. It lasted all Saturday and Sunday before the opening night on the Monday. The musical had been taken off and the advance bookings were good, so everyone was confident of success.

Jocelyn realised Aubrey's wisdom in making her walk on. Her long, flowing dress with its high waist and hanging sleeves took practice to manipulate gracefully. Her houppelade, the conical headdress of the period, shaped like a candle extinguisher, gave her a headache in both senses. She had to remember it had added at least a foot to her height when passing through curtains and flats.

Greatly daring, she sent Dorian a bunch of white heather on the first night, with a card attached wishing him good luck. She signed herself, 'Jocelyn.' Flowers and telegrams were coming in all day. Esme's dressing room looked like a florist's shop. Even Melisande did not have as many as she did. Tension grew after the brief run-through of words in the morning, and though they were all very tired they were strung to a high pitch of excitement which made it impossible for them to relax.

Jocelyn took a short walk in the afternoon and came

to the theatre early. Melisande arrived in good time, to everybody's relief, accompanied by Dorian; he had not let her out of his sight since the morning rehearsal, fearing first-night nerves might drive her to seek stimulation.

Standing in the wings to watch her principal make her first entrance, Jocelyn became aware of Dorian's presence behind her. He looked magnificent in a crimson fur-trimmed tunic, on which were quartered the lions of England and the lilies of France, the Plantagenet insignia. His shapely legs were displayed in the close-fitting hose of the period, and around his neck was a massive gold collar, fastened with the red rose of Lancaster in rubies. A linked golden belt girdled his narrow hips, in which was thrust a jewelled dagger. Precious stones and metals were all cleverly faked, and the fur was only humble rabbit, but the effect was rich and sumptuous. His hair, nearly shoulder-length beneath the ducal circlet, was its natural colour; he had refused to dye it, although the Plantagenets were supposed to be fair men.

'Thank you for the heather,' he whispered. 'It was a nice thought. Reminded me of Scotland.' And to her startled surprise, he squeezed her shoulder with fingers glittering with rings before passing on to the stage.

A casual gesture, but Jocelyn went away to dress for her own appearance in the next act feeling absurdly gratified.

There were no hitches; the play had been rehearsed too well for those. One gorgeous scene of mediaeval pageantry followed another, interspersed with shorter more intimate ones. The love theme predominated, and Melisande's appealing beauty complemented Dorian's magnificent presence, his fiery passion made its impact. From first to last there was no doubt that the play was going over well, and the sustained applause at the final curtain confirmed its success.

Dorian Armitage was given a standing ovation, after the curtain call. The circle and pit stamped and shouted for him with all the abandon of pent emotion finding release. He had taken them with him back into a past age and revealed to them a fine, contradictory but very human character, who, though long dead, had lived again that night.

Back stage Jocelyn met Dame Eleanor on the staircase leading up to the meaner dressing rooms. She had changed after her brief appearance and had returned to fetch her coat before hurrying home.

'Dame Eleanor, have you lost your way?' she asked, for the stars' dressing rooms were at floor level.

'No, I was coming to look for you,' the old lady said. 'What do you think of our Dorian now? He's never given a finer performance.'

'He was marvellous.' Jocelyn's eyes shone. 'I went round in front to watch the last act, and Dorian's acting completely carried me away.'

Dame Eleanor was dabbing her eyes, for she had been crying with emotion and relief.

'It'll have a long run,' she predicted. 'But, child, I wish you'd been playing instead of the die-away Melisande. Oh, she looked lovely and I suppose she was adequate, but she has no fire.'

Jocelyn thanked her; she had thought herself that she could have put much more into the part.

'But nothing mattered except Dorian,' she declared.

'Fire strikes fire,' Dame Eleanor said. 'I'd like to see you and Dorian play together. The Constanza was very good, she's meant to be cold and unsympathetic, but Esme was awful, a barmaid trying to portray a duchess.'

'You shouldn't be standing here in the draughts,' Jocelyn told her, looking round uneasily to see if anyone had overheard her companion's forthright remarks. 'Can't I take you to Dorian's dressing room?'

'I've just come from there; there's such a crush you can't get near him. There's to be a bottle party to celebrate and I've come to ask you to join us.'

Jocelyn was touched. 'It's very sweet of you to think of me,' she said, 'but I'm not dressed for a party and I couldn't get home afterwards—besides, I'm too unimportant to mix with the V.I.P.s.'

'Nonsense!' the old lady exclaimed energetically. 'Most of the cast's been invited and nobody will be dressed up. I'll see you get transport. Dorian wants you to come.'

'Dorian?' Jocelyn nearly dropped her coat and bag in her surprise. Except for those few words tonight, Dorian had been as remote from her as the stars after which his status was named ever since he had come to the Paragon.

'Yes.' Dame Eleanor sounded a little impatient. 'Now come along without any more argument. Please give me your arm, I'm stiff with sitting so long and need support.'

A little dashed, as she supported the old woman through the theatre, for it seemed Dorian wanted her merely to look after his grandmother, Jocelyn conducted her to the stage door.

Cars were waiting for the principals outside, and also a crowd of fans. Dame Eleanor had hired a vehicle complete with chauffeur for the occasion and she pointed it out to Jocelyn.

'If we can get to it through this mob, but at least we'll get away before Dorian comes out. He's going to be held up some time.' Paper and pencils were being waved by hopeful autograph-hunters. 'I'll arrange with the driver to take you home when it's over.'

'It's some way out,' Jocelyn demurred, for she lived in the southern suburbs.

'I didn't imagine you lived in Trafalgar Square,' Dame Eleanor snapped, for she was very tired. Not recognising her, and deciding they were not celebrities, the crowd let them through.

As she settled herself in the back of the car, the old lady said:

'It'll be a different story one of these days, you won't escape so easily.'

Jocelyn was grateful for her benefactress's continuing faith in her, but she wondered if that day would ever come.

The supper room slowly filled up while they waited for Dorian, as the members of the cast appeared. Dame Eleanor had calmly seated herself next to the table reserved for the principals, and bade Jocelyn sit beside her. Esme Carr came in, having found time to make an elaborate toilet, but most of the guests wore their ordinary street clothes. She was escorted by a stout and prosperous-looking individual, who was one of the sponsors. Seeing Jocelyn, she demanded:

'What's that girl doing there? That table's reserved for notables.'

Dame Eleanor raised her lorgnette and stared at her.

'Miss Seymour kindly consented to look after me,' she said in her clear carrying voice. 'I don't know what I'd do without her.'

'Oh, Dame Eleanor,' Esme gushed, while looking daggers at Jocelyn. 'I didn't know you were alone. If only you'd asked me!'

'I didn't have to ask, she offered,' the old lady was calmly mendacious. 'She found me lonely and neglected backstage while you were receiving homage from your admirers with no thought for anybody but yourself.'

She looked pointedly at Esme's escort.

'Such a shame she hasn't got any,' Esme sneered, as Aubrey came up to them in time to hear her words.

'She will have one day,' he remarked coolly. 'More than you've ever achieved, Esme darling. May I sit with you, Dame Eleanor?'

The old lady beamed at him as she gave permission, pleased that he had snubbed Esme. The actress moved away scowling, while he asked Jocelyn what she had thought of the way the play had gone, for all the world as if her opinion were important to him.

When at last Dorian came in they all spontaneously rose to their feet and gave a cheer. He looked pale and drained, but his eyes glowed with triumph and satisfaction. With his long hair he still looked slightly mediaeval in spite of his lounge suit. Melisande was clinging to his arm and gazing up at him with near adoration. Her short simple dress made her look like a child; though he was not exceptionally tall, great height would have been a disadvantage in his profession; her extreme slenderness made her look diminutive besides him, and his attitude towards her was protective.

'A clinging vine,' Dame Eleanor snorted in an undertone. 'Catherine Swynford was never that!'

Dorian stopped to speak to his grandmother, but his eyes were on Jocelyn. She saw that he was wearing in his buttonhole a spray of white heather, and hardly dared to believe it was her heather.

He passed on to the place of honour amid laughter and congratulations. Champagne was served and everyone became very gay, as they toasted Dorian, the ladies of the company, the principal men, a long run for the play and many other things.

Jocelyn thought Dame Eleanor was looking very exhausted and suggested they should leave. The old lady was loth to go, she hated to feel she was missing anything, but Aubrey, who had also noticed her pallor, insisted. He tried to help them to leave unobtrusively, but it was not easy without causing a slight stir. As they reached the door they found Dorian beside them.

'You've overdone it, Gran,' he said reproachfully,

'you should be in bed.' He looked at Jocelyn appealingly. 'Could you go home with her, and as it's so late, perhaps you would stay the night?'

'I'm not in my dotage yet!' Dame Eleanor was indignant. 'But I'd be glad if you would stay, Jocelyn.'

'I'd be pleased to,' Jocelyn agreed. She had a standing arrangement with a hostel where she could spend the night if she was too late for her last train, and her people would not worry.

Dorian gave her his most charming smile.

'That's a good girl,' he said gratefully.

He insisted upon coming with them to the car, offering his arm to his grandmother. Arrived at the vehicle he helped them both into the back of it.

'Take care of her,' he said to Jocelyn. 'She's very precious.' He sighed. 'I wish I could come with you instead of having to go back to that racket in there.'

'Why don't you?' Dame Eleanor asked.

'It wouldn't do, would it, as the party's being given in my honour.'

He seemed softer and gentler than Jocelyn had ever known him to be, and the eyes that rested upon her were kind.

He stepped back as the car moved off and waved to them from the pavement. In spite of his triumph, the popular acclaim of both the public and his colleagues, Jocelyn thought he looked oddly lonely and a little sad.

She herself was elated. Dorian seemed to have got over his former animosity, and in the morning she would see Dorry.

'He's forgiven me!' she exclaimed joyfully.

'Forgiven you?' Dame Eleanor echoed. 'Whatever did he have to forgive? Oh, you mean that silly idea of marrying you, which you so sensibly refused.' She settled herself more comfortably in her corner. 'He'll have forgotten all about that now he's chasing Melisande.' She closed her eyes.

It seemed to have slipped her mind that the silly idea had originally been hers. Some of Jocelyn's elation seeped away.

'Is he serious about her?' she asked hesitantly.

'Oh, lord, I hope not.' Dame Eleanor opened her eyes and sat up with a jerk. 'Whatever gave you that idea?'

'Well, if he's smitten,' Jocelyn began uncertainly. 'He's more gentle with her than I've ever seen him with anybody.'

Except the old lady beside her and occasionally his son, but he had never shown herself any gentleness.

'The boy has some chivalry, you know,' the old lady said a little sharply. 'Melisande's frailty arouses his best impulses.'

'And pity is akin to love,' Jocelyn murmured.

'As for that, he always maintains that a personal relationship with his leading lady helps to make the love scenes convincing.' She gave her throaty chuckle.

Which substantiated what Esme had said.

'Compassion is one thing, marriage another,' Dame Eleanor went on, betraying that Jocelyn's observations had produced some anxiety in her. 'But he must know that the nature of that girl's weakness precludes marriage. Surely he wouldn't be such a fool as to involve himself in a second tragedy?' She sighed. 'I suppose it's inevitable that Dorian will fall heavily for somebody, and the wrong sort of mate seems to have a fatal fascination for him.'

Jocelyn found this conversation a little painful, her companion seemed to have forgotten that her own heart was involved, or had she never believed it was so? She remembered the way Melisande had looked at Dorian. She was caught if he was not—what a muddle it all was! She said lightly:

'If only Oberon's little western flower was a reality.

Perhaps some day scientists will invent a chemical that will ensure that every Jack falls for the right Jill and vice versa.'

'Which would deprive writers of their principal source of material,' Dame Eleanor pointed out. She began to nod sleepily. 'Don't forget that even in *The Dream* the wrong people got the treatment. You'll never dispense with love tangles.' She yawned. 'As Puck says in the same play, "Lord, what fools these mortals be!"'

And none more foolish then herself, Jocelyn thought, to continue to hanker after Dorian, who did not want her and was engrossed in his glamorous leading lady.

The critics were enthusiastic about *Time-Honoured Lancaster*. Such a joy, they wrote, to be given a serious play without smut or gimmicks with good sound acting. Dorian was lauded to the skies. The others given a bare mention. The audience too was praised for being able to appreciate a fine performance, it showed public taste was not yet entirely debased.

Aubrey rubbed his hands gleefully over the box office returns and the company settled down for a long prosperous run.

A fortnight after the opening night, Melisande Everett was unfit to play her part. She arrived at the theatre obviously incapacitated and passed out in her dresser's arms. This happened when the quarter of an hour had been called, giving little time to fill the breach. An ambulance was called, Jocelyn was summoned and had to dress hurriedly and make up with Melisande lying on the couch behind her looking like a corpse.

Fortunately Catherine's first dress was easy, a simple flowing gown with no elaborate headdress. In the opening scene Catherine has to appear young and gauche, when she is introduced to the court and engaged as one of the Duchess of Lancaster's waiting ladies.

A further contretemps was caused by Esme Carr. She went storming to Aubrey, protesting that that amateur, as she styled Jocelyn could not possibly be entrusted with the part. She would ruin Dorian's performance. She herself had learned the words, for she knew Melisande's reputation and had foreseen this eventuality, and if any understudy went on tonight, she declared, it must be hers. Aubrey was diplomatic. Esme might know the lines, but she had never rehearsed the moves. Jocelyn had and she must go on tonight. Tomorrow, if Melisande were still 'unwell', Esme could rehearse it, though he did not promise, and with that she had to be content.

Curtain rise was a little late as the result of all this, and a certain uneasiness pervaded the company. Most of Jocelyn's early scenes were with Esme, and the actress was as spiteful as only an experienced player knew how to be. She upstaged her, deliberately moved during her most important lines to distract the audience's attention from her, cut into her lines and gave wrong cues. This made heavy going for poor Jocelyn, already filled with nervous anxiety. Somehow she got through, but she was far from her best. Only one scene had gone well, the one where she first met John. With Dorian on stage, Esme had not dared to try any tricks.

At the end of her act, as Jocelyn went towards her dressing room filled with despair, an old actor, Jasper Keyne, who was playing the aged King Edward, intercepted her with consoling words.

'You didn't have a chance, my dear. Jealousy is the curse of our profession, but Esme Carr is the greatest bitch of all time.'

'I suppose if I'd had more experience I could have coped.' Jocelyn said wearily.

'I doubt it, but cheer up, you'll do fine in the next act, I'm sure.'

Jocelyn was not so certain. Most of her scenes would be with Dorian, but would he give her the confidence she so sorely needed? He must be feeling upset and anxious about Melisande and she had not had a chance to speak to him privately beforehand. He might resent her as much as Esme did, and though he would not descend to her tactics, he might be afraid her inexperience would spoil his own performance. Aubrey had made a mistake, he should have let Esme play the part. How she wished she and Dorian could have had a run-through together before she was precipitated literally into his arms, for most of the scenes were love scenes.

She need not have worried. Dorian was wonderful to act with. The few occasions when she fumbled he covered up for her, but as the act progressed they found themselves en rapport. New confidence flowed through her and together they swept to a mutual summit of power and passion, wherein Dorian surpassed all previous performances.

The act ended with the scene that she had read at her audition, in which John tells Catherine that he is for political reasons about to marry the heiress to Castile. Catherine was depicted in the play as completely unmercenary; all she feared was the loss of John's love. Though hating what must be, and carrying his child, Catherine has to submit. The act ends with John's assertion:

'Come what may, I shall love you till I die.'

Only acting, but splendid acting. Jocelyn went to change between the acts with the passionate sincerity of his last words ringing in her ears. She had so thoroughly identified with her part, they seemed to be true. Two people had told her that Dorian liked to be a little in love with his leading lady as it helped his interpretation of his role. After tonight could he continue to be indifferent to her?

The last act was their parting. After ten years of passionate love life, circumstances became too much for them. John went back to his Spanish wife, and Catherine to her estate in Lincolnshire—this was an historical fact vouched for by a recorded quit claim. But their story did not end there. Constanza died a decade later, and the following year Catherine's children were legitimated—an unprecendented act by Pope and king, on condition that the lovers were married. The elevation of the governess to be Duchesss of Lancaster had all the romantic appeal of the Cinderella story, and this happy ending, rare in historical plays, was partly responsible for this one's popularity.

Jocelyn was anxious about this last act. In it she had to portray a mature woman; Catherine was forty-five when she married John, and the mother of a family. Make-up made the alteration to her face, and she acted with quiet dignity, subduing her earlier fire. When the curtain descended, Dorian turned to her and said quietly:

'Well done.'

Then the applause came. An announcement had been made before the play started apologising for Melisande's non-appearance and the audience had been prepared to accept a mediocre presentation, overshadowed by Dorian's. They were delightfully surprised, and when Dorian led her in front of the curtain, they expressed their appreciation in thunderous applause.

Dorian, gorgeous in the purple velvet robe trimmed with ermine which he had worn in the last scene, kissed her hand, then suddenly the strain and tension under which they had been working snapped. Jocelyn swayed towards him and he took her in his arms in a spontaneous gesture of gratitude and relief. The delighted audience cheered wildly, the whole theatre united in a moment of intense emotion.

It was over; back behind the tabs, Dorian dropped her hand, and actually apologised for being carried away. Aubrey insisted she must take a solo call, and the unwelcome thought occurred to her that she had stolen some of Dorian's thunder. Jasper Keyne had told her after the first act, which now seemed like a nightmare that had happened a long time ago, that actors were jealous folk. When she finally disappeared, and the lights lowered on the stage to indicate that the fun was over, Dorian had disappeared. She was reminded then that he was not her lover, but the cynical actor who had played such havoc with her feelings and had asserted that she was too immature to be entrusted with the part that she had played so triumphantly that night.

Aubrey Oliphant followed her into her dressing room and kissed her without inhibition.

'Tonight a star has been born,' he told her solemnly.

Why could not Dorian have said something like that?

'It's been wonderful,' she sighed. 'What are you going to do about Esme? Will she play it tomorrow night?'

'Will she hell, and if she behaves like she did tonight, she'll find herself out of the cast,' he said firmly. 'And since Melisande has put herself out of court, the part's yours, darling, for the rest of the run.'

Jocelyn should have felt jubilant, but she was sobered by the thought of Melisande. Since indisposition was an euphemism for what had been wrong with her, she could be dismissed, but would Dorian stand for that? Wouldn't he insist that she was given another chance? It seemed he must be having regrets, for although all the cast crowded round her, when she was dressed and ready to go home, to congratulate her—

except Esme, of course—he held aloof. She caught a glimpse of him talking to Aubrey on her way out. She paused, uttering a timid 'Goodnight', for now surely he would say something to her.

'Goodnight, Jocelyn,' he turned casually, throwing her an unfathomable glance, and turned back to Aubrey.

He had said 'Well done', but that was before the audience had expressed their enthusiasm. She could not bring herself to believe that he was so petty as to begrudge her her triumph, but he was definitely displeased, possibly upon Melisande's account. Her pleasure in her success was marred, and the situation was not improved when Jasper Keyne, who was following her, remarked tactlessly:

'You'll have to watch out, my boy, or she'll steal your laurels!'

Outside she found a crowd of young people were waiting to waylay her, and she had her first experience of signing autographs. When she was through, weary and spent, it was Aubrey who came out to rescue her, Aubrey who put her in a taxi, saying she must charge it up to expenses, and continued to express his approbation. Of Dorian there was no sign.

CHAPTER NINE

Time-Honoured Lancaster settled down for a long run with Jocelyn continuing to play Catherine. There had been an unpleasant scene with Esme when Aubrey had told her straight that he would never allow her to appear in the part, and if she were not satisfied with what she had got he would be pleased to release her from her contract. Esme elected to stay, but Jocelyn was never comfortable in her scenes with her, for her hostility was never wholly disguised.

For the rest, as nightly Catherine and John—Jocelyn and Dorian—simulated passionate love the evenings were bitter sweet interludes for the girl. Her performance increased in polish and depth, but apart from the play she saw little of her stage lover, for Dorian continued to hold aloof, and she surmised that he could not wholly forgive her for being more successful than the unfortunate Melisande. To come together night after night except Sundays, after dreaming of him all day, was a strange existence. So ardent was he on stage that it was with difficulty that she could persuade herself of his indifference. He had become so identified with his part, she was always expecting reciprocation.

When the Christmas holidays started, she called frequently at Dame Eleanor's Hampstead flat, since the old lady had given her a standing invitation, for the purpose of seeing Dorry. She took him out upon several occasions to show him the sights of London, but she never went there on Sundays, for that was Dorian's day with his son.

Dorry was becoming a typical schoolboy, his French expressions being replaced by English slang. He had not yet seen his father act, and was to be taken to a matinee during the holidays.

During one of Jocelyn's visits, Dame Eleanor let slip that Dorian was paying the fees for the expensive sanatorium where Melisande was staying.

'The girl hasn't a bean of her own,' she explained. 'Improvident, like most artistes.' Her brow creased in a worried frown.

'Will she be cured?' Jocelyn asked.

'You can never be sure with that affliction, but her stage career is finished, and that's what's bothering me. Dorian can be absurdly quixotic. He keeps saying Melisande would be all right if she had a good home. I'm afraid he's contemplating marrying her.'

'But Dorry—she wouldn't be the right stepmother for him,' Jocelyn said faintly. She had never imagined Dorian could be quixotic, but apparently his grandmother knew a different side of him from the one with which she was familiar. But to marry Melisande would surely spell disaster and she could appreciate Dame Eleanor's anxiety apart from the personal pain her words had caused herself.

'He thinks Dorry would be a stabilising influence. Unlike Elise, Melisande adores children, and with her heritage she ought not to have any. Dorry could compensate her for that deprivation. The decisive factor is that she has left the stage. Dorian always swore he would never marry an actress, theatrical marriages so frequently break up.'

Jocelyn remembered that Dorian had told her she must give up her profession if she married him. If he had offered out of love, she might have been prepared to do so, and she was then unknown. Now success had increased the distance between them, for it would be much harder to give up now, but that sacrifice would never have to be made, for Dorian would never ask her to do it, he did not love her and was considering marrying Melisande.

As regards her future, she would have no difficulty now in obtaining engagements. She had already had several tentative offers, but she could not bear to look beyond the run of *Time-Honoured Lancaster*. Her life was lit by the sun of Dorian's presence, and without him it would become dark indeed.

Christmas came and went with little respite for the players beyond the one day's rest. An extra matinee was given on Boxing Day, for even the competition of the pantomimes did not diminish the popularity of the play. Jocelyn spent Christmas Day quietly at home. She had given Dorry a toy she knew he desired and sent flowers to Dame Eleanor. She would have liked to present Dorian with a gift, but did not quite dare. She ventured upon a card and received one from him, but so did all the rest of the company.

Dorry came to a matinee of the play and was conducted back stage afterwards, to meet his father and herself. He had not been able to follow the plot, but he was impressed by the pageantry, and being sensitive had been moved by their puzzling emotions. He could not reconcile Jocelyn or his father with the gorgeous figures on the stage, and kept saying to her:

'Was that really you?'

He confided to her that he had much preferred the pantomime he had seen on Boxing Day, when King Rat had invaded the stalls where he was sitting and been chased away by Dick Wittington's cat.

'That was super,' he sighed.

The stage manager took him up into the flies, while he waited for Dame Eleanor to finish talking to Dorian, before taking him home, and showed him how the tabs were raised and lowered. That he found a great deal more interesting than the play.

January came in wet and cold and started an epidemic of 'flu coughs and colds. There was a Saturday evening when Dorian was obviously making a great effort to stay upon his feet. He got through, though only Jocelyn knew how bad he was, his hands when he touched her seemed burning hot. Aubrey told him jocularly to go home and spend Sunday in bed with a whisky bottle.

'Got anybody to look after you?' he enquired.

'My usual woman, actually she's the caretaker. Don't worry, I'll be all right on Monday.'

But he was not. The company was notified that the theatre would close for a week. Since Dorian was ill, as Gordon Thomas had predicted, the management decided that nobody could satisfactorily take his place.

On the Thursday of that week, Jocelyn paid a visit to Hampstead. She had been unable to obtain any news of Dorian; nobody seemed to know how he was faring, and if Aubrey knew anything, he kept his own counsel. Jocelyn half expected to find him with his grandmother, and if that were so she would make her enquiries and depart without going in. What she did find was Dame Eleanor confined to the house with a bronchial cough, Dorry with a streaming cold, but no Dorian ...

'I'm worried to death about him,' the old lady confided to her. 'He's at his flat, but I've rung and rung without getting any reply. That woman who looks after him, Mrs Jenks or whatever she's called, might answer if he can't, but I'm sure she's neglecting him. I mustn't go out myself, or I'd go and see what's happening. Now you've providentially turned up, would you go?'

'I?' Jocelyn was taken aback. 'Go to Dorian's flat?'

'Don't I speak plain? You can at least ascertain why he doesn't answer the telephone.'

'Perhaps he isn't there,' Jocelyn said faintly.

'Then where is he? Aubrey insists he's at home and was merely facetious when I asked him to go and see. He says half the company is smitten, including, thank goodness, Esme, and he can't act wet nurse to all of them. He implied that Dorian probably had his reasons for not wanting interruptions.'

'When did you last hear from him?' Jocelyn asked, wincing at this imputation. Could Melisande possibly be there?

'Last Sunday morning, he rang up to say he couldn't come as usual. Jocelyn, he may be seriously ill without anybody knowing.'

'But surely this Mrs Jenks would have let you know?'

'She may be ill too. Jocelyn, you must go.'

But Jocelyn was unwilling to intrude; she had no idea what her welcome would be, or what embarrassing situation she might blunder into.

'If you won't go, I'll have to venture myself, and risk pneumonia,' Dame Eleanor said desperately.

'No, you mustn't do that,' Jocelyn protested hastily. The old woman coughed incessantly and was certainly not fit to go out. Anxiety is catching, and in spite of her reluctance Jocelyn was beginning to feel worried. There was probably some good reason for Dorian's silence, but there was also the possibility that something was seriously wrong.

So she let herself be persuaded, reflecting that Dame Eleanor's anxiety was a sufficient excuse for calling upon him. If he were quite all right, he would have only his own thoughtlessness to blame for her intrusion and she would tell him so.

Having got her way, Dame Eleanor insisted that Jocelyn went armed with a bag of provisions and a dozen fresh eggs—they were special, she declared, having been delivered that morning from a farm—lemons, barley water and various other items.

'What shall I do with it all, if he isn't there?' Jocelyn asked, embarrassed by this largesse.

'Oh, take it home or give it to someone in the street, but he'll be there.'

Thereupon she rang for a taxi, anxious to set Jocelyn upon her way as quickly as possible and without giving her time to change her mind.

'I'll pay for it,' she said generously.

That Jocelyn would not allow; she was earning a much increased salary since her promotion.

Dorry protested loudly at Jocelyn's precipitate departure and demanded to 'come too.' But he was no more fit to go out than his grandmother, though Jocelyn would have been glad to take him as a bulwark against Dorian's possible displeasure. Leaving the old lady to pacify him, she went out to the taxi, with Dame Eleanor's parting injunction.

'Ring me as soon as you can.'

Jocelyn promised.

Dorian lived in an expensive apartment block not far from Kensington Gardens. Dismissing the taxi, Jocelyn approached the impressive-looking building somewhat diffidently. A notice board in the entry informed her that D. Armitage's flat was on the first floor. The caretaker was located in the basement. She thought of contacting her first, then scorned herself for her shyness. She had a perfectly legitimate excuse for calling upon Dorian. Disdaining the lift for such a short journey, she ran up the stairs and found Dorian's number. She rang the bell, but no one came to open the door, nor could she detect any sign of movement from within. Repeated ringing produced no response. So Dorian was not at home, which would explain why he had not answered his telephone. But she did not want to leave without delivering Dame Eleanor's gifts. Dorian must return some time. Expecting to find it locked, she tried the door handle, and to her surprise it opened. Pushing it ajar, intending to deposit the bag inside, she saw several milk bottles left on the mat, apparently the reason why the door was not fastened, a scattering of mail and daily papers. She frowned at them uneasily. She had meant to deposit her load and depart, but there was something ominous about those milk bottles. If he were away, why had not he stopped delivery? He might have forgotten, but then he would have locked the door before leaving. She had read so many reports of cases where milk bottles had been the evidence of tragedies that they had come to have a sinister connotation. She set down the bag of provisions and looked about her.

Coats were hanging in the lobby, which she recognised as Dorian's, including the one he always wore to the theatre, sure evidence that this was his domicile. A passage led out of it, apparently running the length of the flat, for there were doors on either side of it. One, a little way down it, was open a crack with a shaft of light issuing from it, piercing the winter dusk that was beginning to gather in the corridor. Somebody appeared to be there, but why had not he or she answered the door? A chill foreboding assailed her; there was something uncanny about the silence enfolding her. She called out, and her voice sounded shrill and strange.

'Is there anybody at home?'

From the room where the light showed, she heard the clink of glass, and a husky voice replied:

'Is that you, Jenks, at last? Why the devil did you keep on ringing? I left the door unlocked for you.'

She advanced a little way down the passage before saying:

'I'm not Mrs Jenks.'

'Then for God's sake get out, and let me alone!'

Oddly enough this harsh command caused Jocelyn's trepidation to vanish. It was Dorian's voice, and she deduced that he was expecting his domestic help, who had obviously not returned from wherever she had gone. Probably he was in need of assistance which she could render, so she went boldly up to the door and pushed it open. What it revealed filled her with dismay.

The room was a good-sized one, elegantly furnished, but in an indescribable state of chaos. A cupboard door hung open, disclosing an array of bottles. Dirty glasses were on the polished tables and whatnots; dying chrysanthemums wilted in a vase; discarded clothing was flung anyhow on the Chippendale chairs.

In an armchair in front of an electric fire burning full blast in spite of the central heating, Dorian sat huddled in a dressing gown, an eiderdown over his knees, his face flushed and unshaven, his eyes fever-bright. The heavy atmosphere smelt of spirits and a whisky bottle and tumbler on the table beside him betrayed its source. For one shocked moment she wondered if he were drunk.

'Dorian!' she gasped, horrified.

He stared at her blankly, then passed his hand over his eyes.

'God Almighty,' he muttered. 'I'm seeing things.' He stared again. 'Go away, Catherine, I'm not fit to make love to you, much as I should like to. You'll have to come another day.' He laughed feebly, and the laughter ended in a fit of coughing.

'My dear!' Jocelyn was across the room in a flash, laying her cold hand against his forehead. It was very hot. 'You're very ill. You ought to be in bed.'

His burning fingers closed round her wrist and he smiled wryly. 'It's not made, never could make beds. Jenks has gone to her sister, who's having a baby. From the way she went on, you'd think a miracle had occurred ... Lots of women like that with babies ... Elise wasn't ... she didn't want one ... mad with me because she was pregnant ... but she took Dorry away ... Shouldn't have let her ... Dorry's my kid.'

He was rambling. Wondering how long he had been alone and in this state, she asked:

'When did she go?'

'Sunday morning. The child who is born on the Sabbath day ... how does it go, Catherine?'

'Never mind.' So no one had been near him since last Sunday. Appalled by his condition, she wondered what to do. Since the caretaker was still away there was no one to whom she could apply for help. She could telephone, if it were working, but first Dorian should be put in bed and the doctor summoned—that she was quite capable of doing herself.

'Good thing I came,' she said briskly. 'I'll soon put things to rights.' She tried to disengage her hand.

He refused to relinquish it, pulling her towards him.

'Please let me go, Dorian,' she besought him quietly. 'There's so much to do.'

'No, I won't let you go. This time I've got you,' he announced triumphantly, his eyes glittering like emeralds. 'You've come before, but when I called to you you disappeared.' He drew her on to his knees, and his other hand closed about her waist. 'My love, my Catherine ... I'll never let you go.'

'I don't want to go, but please darling be sensible.'

She was inwardly quaking. He seemed to be delirious and she did not know how to cope with him. 'You must let me make you more comfortable,' she pleaded.

His head drooped against her breast, the rough dark locks, grown long for John, brushed her chin. He gave a long sigh.

'Comfortable ... like this.'

'Not really. Wouldn't you like a cool drink?'

That diverted him.

'Whisky ... good for a cold.' He reached for the

tumbler and she slipped out of his grasp.

She made a hurried inspection of the premises. His bedroom was next door, the bedclothes tumbled on the floor, the sheet stained with spilt coffee. The kitchen was further along, its immaculateness marred by the debris of a meal several days old. Evidently he had not prepared any food recently. She knew he had most of his meals out, but he had not been fit to go out.

In a cubbyhole next to the lobby she found the telephone with the receiver off the hook. So that was why Dame Eleanor had not been able to contact him.

She returned to Dorian. 'As soon as I've made the bed you're going straight into it,' she told him, 'and then I'm going to ring the doctor. What's his name?'

He shrugged his shoulders. 'I don't want a doctor. I've only got a bit of a cold.'

'Rather more than a bit. You're running a high temperature ... and no more of that!' She seized the whisky bottle.

'Best thing for a cold.'

'In moderation perhaps, but you seem to have been living on it. Why didn't you ring for someone to come to you?'

He shook his head. 'Didn't want any damned women fussing round. Ringing up all the time ... Dor, darling, how are you? Women I've never heard of, or if I had I've forgotten. So I took the receiver off.'

'I wonder no one reported it. But this woman's going to fuss all right.' Misgiving struck her. 'Perhaps you ought to go to hospital.'

That roused him. 'Don't you dare to try and send me away, I won't go. I've only got a bit of a cold. Soon get over it now you've come.'

'Very well. Where do you keep you clean sheets?'

He did not appear to understand her. The airing cupboard in the bathroom seemed the likeliest place and there she found them. Swiftly she made the bed and found and filled a hot water bottle. When she returned, Dorian was slumped over the fire shivering.

'Come on, darling,' she said firmly, and put her hand under his elbow. 'Into bed with you.'

To her relief he stood up and came docilely as a child. Somehow she managed to remove his dressing gown and settle him in the bed. Once there he gave a long sigh of relief as he stretched himself on the clean sheets. He closed his eyes, only to open them suddenly, as she was about to leave the room.

'You aren't going?'

'No, Dorian, I'll be here as long as you need me.'

He seemed satisfied and she withdrew, feeling elated. Dorian wanted her; in his extremity he had turned to her.

She found a doctor's number on the pad by the telephone, and to her great joy Doctor Brown was in and promised to come at once, when she had named her patient. She fetched a basin of warm water and bathed Dorian's face and hands, which seemed to ease him. He submitted meekly to her ministrations and swallowed one of Dame Eleanor's farm eggs beaten up in milk, but when she set a glass of lemon barley water beside him, he rebelled, eyeing it with disgust, and demanded his whisky.

'No more of that,' she said firmly. 'This will do your throat good.'

He took a sip, made a grimace and gave her a quizzical look.

'Real tyrant, aren't you, nurse?'

'I know what's best for you. Now try to go to sleep.'

'You don't know what's good for me ... you've haunted me,' he said fretfully. 'Tantalising little witch.' He groped for her hand. 'You'll stay with me, Catherine?'

To pacify him she let him hold it, wondering if he really knew who she was. He had not addressed her by name, but had persistently called her Catherine. Melisande had played Catherine too, she had been his choice for the part—had they become confused in his fevered brain? The woman he was contemplating marrying and possibly loved, and the other one who was barred because she had become a successful actress? Jocelyn was tempted to say:

'I'm not Melisande, you know,' and watch his reaction.

But he was in no condition to be so tested. If he found her presence comforting, whoever he thought she was, that was sufficient for the present.

The doctor's arrival released her from her vigil.

She had decided to wait to ring Dame Eleanor until after his visit, and his diagnosis was reassuring. Far from being at death's door, all Dorian had was a bad influenza cold, aggravated by neglect. There was a risk of it turning to pneumonia or pleurisy if he didn't take care, but he was sure Jocelyn would ensure that he did. Penicillin would clear up his condition, and after a day of two in bed he might even be fit to return to the theatre during the following week.

The examination completed, the medicine produced, Jocelyn walked with the doctor to the front door.

'I know that young man,' he told her, 'strong and healthy as a young carthorse, but incapable of taking care of himself when he's under the weather. Would you like me to send a nurse?'

Jocelyn hesitated. 'Does he need professional nursing?'

'Oh, no, just ordinary attention, and you seem very capable. You're ... ahem, staying here?'

Jocelyn made her decision. 'Yes,' she said.

Afterwards she wondered at her own temerity, but at the moment all she felt was that Dorian needed her and she was determined to stay as long as he did so. It was obvious what the doctor thought, but she did not care.

When he had gone and Dorian appeared to be dozing, Jocelyn was at last able to ring Dame Eleanor.

'You've been long enough,' that lady complained. 'I thought you were never going to call. Was the phone out of order?'

'Not really.' Jocelyn told her all that had transpired.

'So like Dorian!' the old lady ejaculated. 'When it comes to illness he's no more sense than Dorry—not as much. Do I understand you intend to stay with him?'

'He can't be left alone,' Jocelyn pointed out. 'His Mrs Jenks seems to have disappeared. There is another bedroom, so I don't see why I shouldn't.' She spoke a little defiantly. 'The doctor said it wasn't necessary to have a professional nurse.'

The silence at the other end of the line recalled to her the enormity of her proposed action.

'It's no use raising objections,' she went on firmly. 'I don't care a hoot about my reputation. I'm here and here I'm staying until he's better.'

Dame Eleanor's chuckle was clearly audible over the wire.

'Good for you,' she said. 'Carry on, child. I didn't know you had it in you.'

Jocelyn went back to her patient and found he was quietly sleeping. She stayed for some time looking down at his beloved face. She had so seldom seen it in repose, the disconcerting eyes closed. Not that he was looking his best with three days' stubble on cheeks and chin, his hair rough and uncombed, but while he was helpless he was hers. She would have to let Ron know that she was staying in town, so he could inform her parents who were not on the phone, and hoped he would not be too curious. She supposed she ought to have tried to make some arrangement for Dorian, either accepting the doctor's offer of a nurse, or contacting some domestic agency to obtain help. But she had no intention of doing either of these things. It was in her nature to want to serve those she loved, and since fate had given her this opportunity to tend Dorian, she was not going to relinquish it. Nor had his grandmother raised any objection.

What Dorian himself would say when he realised that she had established herself unasked in his flat, she could not conjecture, but until Mrs Jenks returned he could not do without her, and the thought of his dependence upon her was sweet. The only person who had any right to query her presence, since Dame Eleanor apparently approved, was Melisande, but as far as Jocelyn knew she was still in her nursing home and not likely to appear upon the scene.

Later in the evening the calls came. As Dorian had said, every woman he had spoken to made his indisposition an excuse to try to contact him, and a lot were fans who had not even done that. Jocelyn told them patiently, and mendaciously, that Mr Armitage had been moved to a private nursing home and the doctor had forbidden its locality to be disclosed. Eventually she had to recourse to Dorian's strategem and left it off the hook.

She hoped none of them would have the audacity to call, but possibly the dead phone would imply, and had implied during the past few days, that the flat was unoccupied.

The spare room, opposite to Dorian's across the passage, was small and a little cramped. Evidently Dorry had occupied it before he went to Scotland, for the bed cover was designed with the pattern of a racing motor car, and there was a pile of children's books. On the dressing table was a framed photograph of Dorian and presumably Elise. Dorry had printed on a slip of paper stuck to the frame: 'Papa and Maman'. In it Dorian looked younger, almost boyish, but not very happy.

Elise had long straight hair, apparently fair, and a pretty, petulant face. Jocelyn studied the very ordinary features for some time, wondering what the girl had had that her loss had so affected her husband.

She dozed fitfully that night, her door ajar in case Dorian woke, but he never moved. She was up early, cleaning the flat and putting things to rights. It was surprising what an amount of dust and confusion three days' neglect could cause. Then she made her preparations for breakfast, blessing Dame Eleanor's provisions, for there was little in the fridge. Towards nine o'clock, Dorian awoke. She heard him stir, and when she went in she found him sitting up and looking about him with puzzled eyes, evidently wondering how he had got to where he was.

She was thankful to see that the flush had gone and though he looked pale and drawn, his eyes were clear and the fever seemed to have abated.

'Good morning,' she said cheerfully. 'I see you're looking more like yourself. I'll just take your temperature and then how about some breakfast?'

He stared at her. 'So it wasn't a dream? You're really here?'

She thought it best to be as matter-of-fact as possible, and she was rejoiced that he had indentified her and not confused her with Melisande as she had feared.

'Yes, I'm here, and it was a good thing I happened to come along before you died of neglect. Now, if you please.'

She advanced with the thermometer in her hand.

'Take that damn thing away!' he commanded.

'Don't be childish,' she said severely.

He opened his mouth to utter a further protest, and she adroitly slipped the glass cylinder between his teeth. She feared he would take it out, but he did not, and with her eyes upon her watch she went on:

'Your grandmother was worried to death about you,

she's not allowed out and you'd made yourself incommunicado. She asked me to call and see how you were. You should have let her know Mrs Jenks wasn't here.'

Gagged, he could not reply to this reproach, but his eyes were eloquent. He was not going to take her rebuke lying down, and the familiar mocking glint was back in his eyes again.

His temperature was only one point above normal and she gave a long sigh of relief.

'Well, am I dying?' he demanded. 'Or may I get up, nurse?'

'You'll stay in bed until you've had some breakfast and the doctor's been.'

'What, is he coming again?'

'Of course.'

'You and he have been having a field day over my helpless body, but...' his eyes glinted, 'I'll get my own back, you'll see.'

'Dorian, you must try to get well,' she said earnestly, 'the play can't go on until you've recovered. The doctor and I are doing our best to get you on your feet again.'

'They say no one's indispensable, but it seems I am,' he remarked complacently. 'Well, nurse, I'll try to be a good patient.' He passed his hand over his chin and a look of horror came into his eyes. 'Good lord, I'm as prickly as a hedgehog!'

'It doesn't matter,' she was beginning, but he interrupted her.

'It damn well does matter. That I should appear before you of all people with a growth of stubble!' Both personal fastidiousness and his vanity were offended. He threw back the bedclothes.

'Dorian, please stay in bed,' she protested.

'But I must go to the bathroom.'

Irrefutable excuse.

'Very well, but be as quick as you can.'

'You like having me under your thumb, don't you, nurse, but I don't intend to stay there, and then...'

'If you want to go to the bathroom, please go, while I get your breakfast. Could you eat an omelette?'

'I could eat a horse!'

'Horseflesh is not on the menu.'

She watched him walk a little unsteadily along the passage, not daring to offer assistance. The flat being centrally heated, he could not take a chill. She surmised he had not eaten for several days, and needed sustenance. She prepared a tray with tea, toast and marmalade, and beat the eggs for the omelette, ready to drop into the sizzling pan as soon as he returned. He was so long that she was beginning to feel uneasy when she heard the soft pad of his slippered feet along the passage.

'Ready, nurse,' he called.

Thank heaven he seemed prepared to accept her in her self-imposed role, and she hoped he would continue to be amenable.

The omelette came up light and fluffy and she hurried with the tray into the bedroom. Dorian was sitting up against his pillows, immaculately shaved, his dark hair combed, but still damp from a shower; clean pyjamas showed under an oriental robe which must have been in the airing cupboard. He smelt of after-shave and eau de cologne. The rich brocaded material reminded her of the costumes he had worn in the play—her stage lover, but never her lover in reality. The very efficiency she was showing now would put him off her, for she believed Dorian liked his women to be clinging, and Melisande was a veritable vine.

'That looks nice,' he said appreciatively, as she set the tray across his knees. 'So you include cooking among your many other talents. Gran was right when she said you were a paragon.'

'Eat it while it's hot,' she bade him, inwardly wincing from the appellation. He had said at Mallaig that paragons left him cold. Had he deliberately used the word to indicate that though circumstances were forcing him to accept her ministrations, he was as suspicious of her motives as he had been then?

'One doesn't need to be a Cordon Bleu to cook an egg,' she pointed out, 'and were you wise to take a shower?'

'Very wise, it was essential.' He smiled at her, a wholly sweet and charming smile without mockery. 'I needed a wash, and it would be hardly respectable for you to give me a blanket bath.'

'It certainly wouldn't,' but she knew she had blushed, and his eyes gleamed wickedly, he was delighted to have disconcerted her.

'Where did the eggs come from?' he enquired. 'I know there weren't any in the fridge. Jenks should have got some in, but I suppose she forgot. Normally I only have breakfast here, which I get for myself. I too can cook an egg, but I fry them.'

She explained about Dame Eleanor's gift.

'Which is why I came in. I didn't know what to do with them.'

'Thank God you did,' he said so fervently that she was highly gratified; he did appreciate what she had done for him.

He was eating with appetite and a little colour had stolen back into his cheeks. Pleased to see the improvement in him, Jocelyn brought him the paper to read while she went to get her own breakfast.

'Oh, by the way,' he called after her, 'if Aubrey rings up, tell him I'll be back on Monday.'

She halted in the doorway. 'Are you sure you'll be fit?'

'Oh, I'll be fit.'

'The doctor may disagree.'

'He'd better not!'

'And until then? Will Mrs Jenks be coming back?'

'How can I say? She never ought to have gone. You aren't going to desert me, nurse? I'll have a relapse.'

'No ... yes, we'll talk about that later,' she said hurriedly, and went into the kitchen.

Dorian was recovering fast, and that being so this brief, sweet intimacy must end.

It was one thing to tend a sick invalid, another to spend a weekend alone with Dorian at his most provocative. Nor did she particularly want Aubrey to know she was there. He would think it was a great joke and spread the news all round the theatre, and Melisande might get to hear of it. Jocelyn had no wish that her impulsive action in staying with Dorian should come between him and his love.

She resolved to wait until the doctor had been, and if he gave his okay that Dorian could be moved, she would insist that he went to spend his convalescence in Hampstead with his grandmother. It was the obvious solution and the wisest.

CHAPTER TEN

DOCTOR BROWN arrived about the middle of the morning, while Jocelyn was making coffee. Dorian had been quiet and submissive, but his eyes had followed her movements about his room as she had tidied it in preparation for the doctor's visit with a mischievous glint in their green-gold depths. Once she asked:

'Does Miss Everett know you're ill?'

'Melly? I don't think so, why should she?'

'I thought someone might have told her.'

'Most of her colleagues seem to have dropped her,' he told her indignantly. 'Poor Melly, but I hope no one has, it might distress her.'

More than likely, Jocelyn thought, and wished she had held her tongue; his concern for Melisande could only hurt her, and it was a subject best avoided, but she was naturally curious about the relationship between them.

'How is he this morning?' the doctor asked as she opened the door.

'Oh, much better.'

She showed him into Dorian's room, and the patient said:

'Out you go, woman. What happens now is strictly man to man.'

They seemed to be entertaining each other, for she heard Dorian's laugh and the doctor's guffaw more than once. Finally, the coffee being made, she knocked on the door and asked if they would like some.

'Bring it along,' Dorian commanded her, 'and you'll

find a flask of cognac in the cupboard in the sitting room, bring that too.'

'But should you?' She looked at Doctor Brown.

'A nip won't hurt him,' that worthy declared. 'Nor me either. It's a raw day.'

She did as requested, and set the tray between them.

'This is what I like to see,' the doctor observed, 'a devoted wife waiting upon her man, and such a pretty wife too.'

Jocelyn's eyes flew to Dorian's face. What had he been telling the good doctor? She met the wicked gleam in the green-gold eyes, and her heart missed a beat. Once before he had pretended they were engaged to save her reputation, but this time he had gone one better.

Her anxious gaze went to the doctor, who was looking positively fatuous. He could not know who she was, for everyone knew the principals in *Time-Honoured Lancaster* were not man and wife.

But Dorian had his explanation ready.

'I've been telling Doctor Brown we've kept our marriage a secret to avoid publicity, but murder will out and he stumbled upon the truth when he found you here.'

'I must say you quite took me in,' the doctor told her. 'From what you said last night, I'd no idea you were Dorian's wife.' He beamed at her. 'No wonder you didn't want a nurse!'

'My wife's very loyal,' Dorian murmured, evidently enjoying himself hugely. 'She wouldn't breathe a word without my permission.'

'But surely you won't be able to keep it dark much longer?' Doctor Brown enquired. 'You both famous people, and ... well, I've seen the play, and very convincing you were. Everyone must believe there's a romance in the offing.'

'Do they?' Dorian grinned. 'They'll be disappointed to discover it's a perfectly legitimate one.'

Jocelyn flushed. 'Don't be horrible, Dorian! You misjudge the public, they love weddings between celebrities.'

'A little of your glittering stardust falls upon them,' the doctor said sententiously, 'but apparently you've defrauded them over yours.'

'Oh, we may have a public one later on just to please our fans,' Dorian remarked airily.

Jocelyn thought he had romanced quite enough. Thanks to his fairy tale, she could not now ask Doctor Brown if he could go to Hampstead. He would think it so odd.

'Dorian is expecting to be back at the theatre next week,' she said. 'Isn't it too soon?'

'Well, he seems to be recovering fast, but it's too early to say. Go easy, my boy, and keep him quiet, Mrs Armitage, if you can. It would be advisable not to go out of doors during this cold weather.' The doctor rose to his feet. 'Thanks for the coffee and the cognac. I'll look in on Saturday and give you my verdict.'

'Can I get up?' Dorian demanded. 'My dear wife is determined to keep me in bed.'

The glance he threw at Jocelyn was a challenge.

'Yes, if you feel like it, but don't overtire yourself.'

Jocelyn walked with him to the door.

'A splendid recovery,' he told her. 'He's as resilient as a rubber ball.'

He kept her chatting for a while upon the doorstep, seeming in no hurry to let her go.

'And take care of yourself,' was his final injunction. 'We mustn't have you knocking up too.'

Jocelyn sped back to the bedroom to find Dorian in his shirt and trousers, putting on his tie.

'You should knock,' he complained as she burst in impetuously.

'I didn't expect you to be up already. What did you

want to go and spin that pack of lies for?' she asked with vexation. 'It really wasn't necessary.'

His tie arranged to his satisfaction, he turned from the mirror to confront her.

'You'll kindly let me be the judge of that,' he returned.

'If you're thinking of my reputation...'

'I'm not,' he interrupted blandly. 'My brain is seething with far more important matters. It's true you do persist in involving yourself in ambiguous situations, and since Doctor Brown says everyone is sure there's something between us, perhaps I should make an honest woman of you.'

'Thank you, but I'll not expect you to put yourself to so much trouble,' she retorted.

He went to the wardrobe, extracted a jacket and very deliberately put it on, while she, almost automatically, started to strip the bed.

'Leave that,' he bade her. 'We'll go into the sitting room, which would be more suitable now I'm recovered. You and I must have a serious talk.'

'Yes,' she agreed. 'We'll have to find someone to look after you until Mrs Jenks chooses to reappear.'

His eyes darkened, the pupils expanding. 'Are you really such a dimwit, Jocelyn?' he asked.

'I'm not so dim that I don't realise this situation could become highly improper ... now you've recovered.' She returned and walked into the sitting room. This showed signs of her industry; it was swept, dusted and polished, the dead flowers removed.

'I'm not sure I have,' he said plaintively, and deliberately coughed, as he followed her. 'I still need attention.' He gazed round the room. 'You have been busy, my darling, but if you leave me all your handiwork will be wasted, it'll soon look as bad as ever.' He looked at her with mock supplication. 'That's what we're going to discuss.'

'Were we?'

She had closed the door and was standing with her back to it. He came up to her, placing his hands againt it on either side of her so that she was imprisoned facing him.

'You've walked into the spider's web, my love,' he said softly. 'I shan't let you go until I've had my wicked way with you.'

He was only half serious, but there was an ominous glitter in his eyes. Though Jocelyn's heartbeats had quickened, she managed to say flippantly:

'What ingratitude! I find you half dead, nurse you devotedly, and in return you threaten to behave like the villain in a melodrama!'

His teeth gleamed as he smiled.

'It could be more than a threat.' His hands went to her shoulders and he shook her gently. 'Jocelyn, Jocelyn, you must have some red blood in you or you couldn't play Catherine like you do. Why do you always cold-shoulder me?'

Her lips quivered and her eyes filled with tears. Turning her head aside from his searching gaze, she said sadly:

'Oh, Dorian, why must you always torment me so?'

He dropped his hands.

'Torment *you*? Good God, girl, it's you who torment me, you tantalising little iceberg. Ever since I found you in my room with Dorry—and incidentally, you seem to make a habit of turning up in my rooms unasked—you've destroyed my peace of mind.'

He began to pace the room. 'Why did you have to be a great actress?' he demanded. 'Why couldn't you be just an ordinary girl who would be content to make a home for me and Dorry? It would be a sin to divorce you from the stage, but I didn't want to marry an actress, they have too much temperament. I hoped——' He stopped and stared at her, 'Yes, I was mean enough to hope you'd turn out to be merely mediocre, but after your success in the play, I knew it would be wrong for you to give up the stage.'

He resumed his perambulations, while Jocelyn gazed at his moving figure trying to assimilate his words. He *had* resented her triumph, but only because he thought it had raised a barrier between them. Incredibly, it would appear he did care for her.

She said hesitantly: 'Some theatrical partnerships last, and I might consider giving up ... for you.'

He strode towards her.

'What did you say? You'd give it up ... for me?'

The colour mounted in her face and she dropped her eyes. Again he grasped her shoulders.

'Look at me,' he commanded. Reluctantly she raised her eyes and he saw in them all that he wanted to know.

'I couldn't accept such a sacrifice,' he told her, 'it wouldn't be fair ... to the public. That is a player's prime duty, isn't it? To think of the public.' He smiled whimsically. 'So we'll just have to chance it. As you say, some theatrical marriages make out.'

'Dorian, do you mean——?'

'Marriage? What else? You've played fast and loose with me long enough, my girl.' He drew her into his arms. 'We'll make what I told the doctor come true.'

She moved her face away from his seeking lips.

'Dorian, I don't understand. Are you really serious? You can't be, when in Scotland you were so ... cruel.'

Holding her against him, he considered her accusation.

'I suppose I was,' he admitted slowly. 'But there were reasons. A little difficult to explain, but you see when we first met the play was foremost in my mind, and when you appeared in that long blue dress with your hair coiled about your ears, I saw the Catherine I wanted for the part. I continued to confuse you with it.

I suppose subconsciously I identified you with her, and I expected to get from you the passionate responses she gave to her lover. But you were innocent, still unawakened, though it took me some time to realise it, it was so unusual in an actress. Frankly, I found your naïveté irritating, and doubted its genuineness. Eventually I had to accept that my Catherine had the potential, but it was not yet developed.' He sighed. 'I knew, if only you would let me, I could make you flower, but I didn't really want to seduce you. That would have been wrong, so between frustration and inner conflict, I was ... cruel, especially after that nasty crack you gave me by the loch.'

'Oh, Dorian——' She laid her cheek against his. 'I shouldn't have said what I did.'

'It was true up to a point,' he told her. 'I *had* been married before, and made a mess of it. I had serious thoughts of making our fake engagement a real one, until Gran's blundering led me to suspect your coldness was assumed to entrap me, so I offered you terms that only a designing hussy would accept, and contrarily your refusal made me angry. Because I wanted you, my darling, and I knew, once we were married, how it would end.'

'Well, I didn't. I thought you might go on being cruel.'

'Not a very high opinion of me, had you, pet? That was partly what exasperated me, you were so determined to make me play the villain. After that I didn't expect to meet you again, but Gran got Aubrey to engage you as Melly's understudy ... what's the matter now? Do my confessions offend you? I'm only trying to explain how our affairs became so tangled.'

For Jocelyn had pulled herself out of his arms and walked away towards the window.

She said coldly with her back to him:

'Your grandmother gave me to understand that you

and Miss Everett were in love and now that she has had to give up the stage, you wanted to marry her.'

'Meddling again!' he exclaimed. 'Really, Gran can be a menace!' He looked quizzically at Jocelyn's unresponsive back. 'All right, then, I did love Melly, if deep compassion can be called love. Once she was down and out all her friends deserted her, but there was never any question of marriage, neither of us ever dreamed of such a thing. Satisfied?'

'Not in the least.' She did not turn round.

He came up behind her and swung her about to face him.

'I believe you're jealous!' he declared triumphantly.

'Frantically,' she confessed. 'Oh, Dorian, you've had so many loves.'

'Not loves, darling,' he corrected her gently. 'Only fancies, and Elise was merely a boy's infatuation. But not only did I fall in love with you, but I've come to love you. There's a difference, you know.'

She met his gaze wonderingly. His face was quiet, almost grave, and his eyes were neither mocking nor glinting but full of a passionate sincerity.

'I thought, from what I read in your eyes just now, you're not indifferent,' he told her almost humbly. 'Was I wrong?'

Jocelyn shook her head. 'I've never been indifferent.'

'Then you disguised your feelings very thoroughly.'

'I didn't, I was sure you'd guessed, but I didn't dare be too ... forthcoming with you. Actually I fell for you when I saw you as Oberon, and you spoilt me for any other man. Now you've become my whole life, my player king.'

She swayed towards him and he enfolded her in a close embrace. Against her ear, he murmured:

'Come what may, I shall love you till I die.'

She recognised the words. John and Dorian—stage

lover and true lover—had become fused into one entity.

But his kiss was longer, closer and more passionate than any he had ever given her upon the stage.

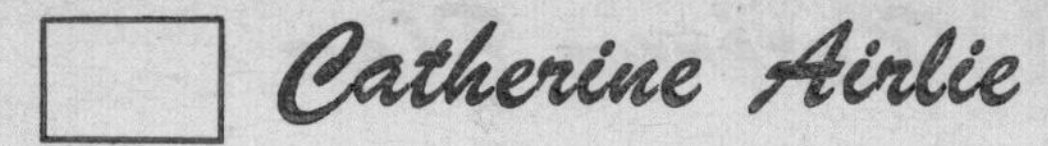
Catherine Airlie

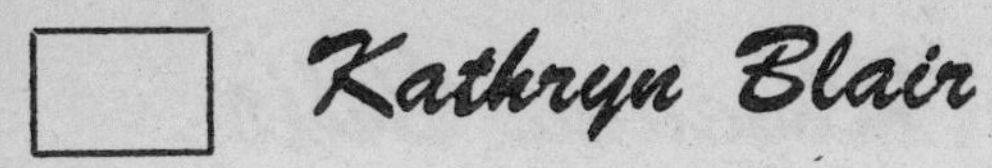

Omnibus

Kathryn Blair's outstanding work has become famous and most appreciated by those who seek real-life characters against backgrounds which create and hold the interest throughout the entire story, thus producing the most captivating and memorable romantic novels available today.

. . . . CONTAINING:

DOCTOR WESTLAND . . . Tess Carlen is invited to recuperate in Tangier after suffering almost fatal injuries in an accident. On the voyage, Tess agrees to look after a small boy, and to deliver him to his father on arrival. By doing so, Tess becomes deeply embroiled in the mystery of Tangier which cloaks Dr. Philip Westland and his young son . . . (#954).

BATTLE OF LOVE . . . on the death of her husband, Catherine and her small son are offered a home by her father-in-law, Leon Verender, co-guardian of the boy. Chaos develops rapidly between them, caused by conflicting ideas on how to raise a child. Leon's scheming fiancée then delivers an ultimatum to Catherine—making life for her and her son impossible . . . (#1038).

FLOWERING WILDERNESS . . . a rubber plantation in Africa was no place for a woman as far as David Raynor was concerned. Nicky Graham had a great deal of courage, and she was determined to stay. Alas, before long, Nicky was forced to leave, but now she was very much in love with the same David Raynor . . . (#1148).

$1.75 per volume

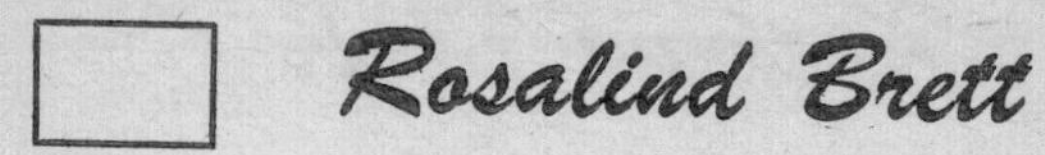

Omnibus

A writer with an excitingly different appeal that transports the reader on a journey of enchantment to far-off places where warm, human people live in true to life circumstances, Miss Brett's refreshing touch to the age-old story of love, continues to fascinate her ever-increasing number of faithful readers.

. . . . CONTAINING:

THE GIRL AT WHITE DRIFT . . . Jerry Lake had travelled from England to Canada to live with her unknown guardian, Dave Farren. On arrival, Mr. Farren drove Jerry to his home, White Drift Farm, explaining that a few months' farm life would strengthen and build a fine body. To her utter horror, Jerry realized that this man thought she was a boy! . . . (#1101).

WINDS OF ENCHANTMENT . . . in Kanos, Africa, in surroundings of intense heat, oppressive jungle, insects and fever, Pat Brading faces the heartbreak of losing her father. The acute depression and shock she suffers in the following months gradually subside, and slowly she becomes aware that she is now married to a man who revolts her and whom she must somehow, escape . . . (#1176).

BRITTLE BONDAGE . . . when Venetia wrote the letter which had brought Blake Garrard immediately to her side in a time of need, she had felt great sorrow and bewilderment. Now, some time and a great deal of pain later, it was the contents of another letter which must drive her away from him. Only now, Blake was her husband . . . (#1319).

$1.75 per volume